A Medical Emergency

A Case for Crabbe and Crabbe

Geoffrey Foster

December 2011

Geoffrey Foster was born in London, England in 1933, and his childhood was mostly spent in the County of Kent, in southeast England. Some of the action of this book, which has occasional echoes of his own experiences, takes place in or around that area and in the suburbs of London.

His father was a policeman most of his working life, and his mother, when she worked, was a shorthand typist (a stenographer). He has two sisters, five and thirteen years younger than himself.

He went to public elementary and secondary school and then to the University of Cambridge, where he studied engineering. Moving to Australia in 1959, he taught Mechanical Engineering at the University of Queensland for 14 years, before switching to educational development, running workshops and other activities for academics. Eventually he took early retirement in 1995.

As well as writing, he likes reading, listening to music, solving cryptic crosswords, walking the family beagle, Kafka, and playing a game with his younger sister, Ynes, that they whimsically refer to as 'tennis.'

Also by Geoffrey Foster:

Kit and the Beeman   ISBN 978-0-9805310-0-8

Kit the Venturer   ISBN 978-0-9805310-1-5

Vincent the Beeman   ISBN 978-0-9805310-2-2

Beatrice's Birthday   ISBN 978-0-9805310-3-9

Beatrice and Vincent's Welsh Adventures

                             ISBN 978-0-9805310-4-6

Trouble at the Mill: A Case for Crabbe and Crabbe

                             ISBN 978-0-9805310-6-0

But is it Art?: A Case for Crabbe and Crabbe

                             ISBN 978-0-9805310-7-7

The Problem with Janice: A Case for Crabbe and Crabbe

                             ISBN 978-0-9805310-8-4

This Book:

A Medical Emergency: A Case for Crabbe and Crabbe

                             ISBN 978-0-9805310-9-1

Chapter 1

When Melpomene and Alex arrived at their agency – 'Crabbe and Crabbe, Private Investigators' – one Monday morning, they found their secretaries, Winnie and Marjorie busily pinning up on the wall the certificates of commendation that the Ambassador of St Luke had presented them with at the Embassy reception the previous evening, to thank them for their contribution to the successful outcome of their case.

As the principals of the firm, Mel and Alex had each been awarded, along with a handsome fee for their services, the medallions of the Order of Saint Luke.

Marjorie said, "We've been thinking we ought to put up our Pitmans' diplomas too – and you two should think about it as well – you always see certificates on professional office walls, and we want to create a reassuring atmosphere for our clients, now we're trying to become more business-like!"

Alex agreed, "You're right – Mel and I should put up our degree certificates, and I should also display my Law Society practicing credentials to show that I'm a solicitor in good standing. Good thinking, Marjorie and Winnie!"

"It is a pity, in my opinion," said Mel, "that there is no requirement for private investigators to be registered, although there have been moves to introduce this. If we wanted to display another certificate, we could join the Association of British Investigators, I suppose – but let's not get too obsessed with all this – we will soon have plenty of work to do on our next case! Has Dr Salmon called yet, Marjorie and Winnie?"

"Oh yes, he did, sorry I forgot to say!" said Winnie, "He asked if ten o'clock would be all right, so I told him it would. There's some mail, too, which we've been through – nothing interesting though, mainly bills – and also adverts for cleaning products, I don't know why!"

Just after ten, Gordon Salmon arrived, carrying a large box file.

"Tea and jam tarts, suit you, Doctor?" asked Winnie, and went to prepare them, while Mel and Alex showed him into the back office and seated him at the conference table. He took papers out of his box, and sorted them into three piles, one large and two smaller.

Winnie popped her head in, saying, "Earl Grey, Lapsang Souchong or ordinary?" Salmon smiled and said that he liked Earl Grey, but wasn't too fussy, "We have to have it out of an urn at the hospital, but, perhaps surprisingly, nobody has died of it yet – as far as I know!"

Alex said, "Gordon, you said you wanted to engage us to investigate a number of matters at your hospital. Two questions – first, do you suspect that there is an organized conspiracy involved here? If so, have you begun to form any conjectures yourself as to which person or persons might be behind it?"

"Perhaps, Melpomene and Alex, I had better begin to explain by referring to my notes, which I have been collecting for more than a year. I have, as you see, divided them into three categories. The tall pile we can set aside for the moment, it consists largely of unresolved incidents where a patient complained that he or she 'could have sworn' that an item was brought into hospital and could no longer be found – like watches, brooches or even purses full of cash – sometimes, I assume, the relatives had taken them home for safe keeping, but I have growing suspicions, based on observations I will explain later, that there is an organised gang of sneak-thieves in action here! But let me first tell you about the other two categories."

He pulled one of the smaller piles closer and said, "This lot I think of as 'medication problems'. These are notes I made at the time of an incident I saw myself, or a report from somebody – I'll read you a typical example, to give you the flavour. Let me see – first, there's the date and time, then it says, '*Mr Smith* (I have his real name recorded) *complains that he was given the wrong medication on one occasion today. He says he is supposed to get half a glass of precipitated chalk in warm water, but was given something that looked the same but tasted very bitter. When he mentioned this to the nurse, she sniffed it, apologized and threw it in the hand-basin. She went off and came back after a few minutes with what he said was the right stuff. I looked at his chart and saw he was in for a gastritis of unspecified aetiology, possibly a peptic ulcer*'. He was not my patient, but he had seen me passing and button-holed me simply because of my white coat and stethoscope. Precipitated chalk is merely a mild antacid, of course. I was in a hurry at the time, so I didn't pursue this with the ward staff. This is somewhat typical of the incidents in this pile, but is rather special because this patient had his wits about him more than most! Many patients take what they are given without question."

"So you never found out what it was that he was given?" asked Mel "No," said Gordon, "I didn't follow it up, I'm afraid, and it had been poured down the drain anyway. I won't go through the whole pile with you – I just wanted to give you a taste. All of the incidents that I have noted here concern – or seem to concern – errors in the administration of medicines or other remedies. In the case of that patient, nothing unfortunate transpired, but in others there were sometimes serious ill-effects, even to the point of fatality. One might expect that all deaths in a hospital would be investigated as a matter of course, but I can tell you that this is not done when the manner of passing seems to be in accord with the patient's ailment. If an elderly woman, who has been suffering with pneumonia and being treated for it, subsequently dies, then the attending physician is likely to give a death certificate accordingly, without calling for an autopsy."

"Are there any common factors in the incidents in this pile?" asked Melpomene, "For instance, are the same people involved in more than one of them?"

"I thought of this," said Gordon, "so after the precipitated chalk incident, I went back to that ward and looked for the nurse, but couldn't tell whether either of the two I saw on duty was the one who 'Mr Smith' had told me about. I asked him, but he said he couldn't be sure, as he wasn't always looked after by the same nurse. On subsequent occasions, I made a point of finding out names when I could. Most of our staff wear name-badges or tags – but often with just their first names. I found that there are three different nurses called 'Ruth' and at least two 'Helens', so in my notes you might see 'bossy Ruth' or 'red-headed Helen'!"

Alex said, "I think we're getting a good idea of what we might find in that pile, Gordon. What about your other small collection – what are those all about? You mentioned your misgivings about the hospital pharmacy – are these to do with that?"

"That's right!" said Gordon, "I'll get onto that next, and try to explain the relationships between the pharmacy and the medical and nursing staff on the wards. I suppose that I and one or two colleagues amount to a special group, who are not allocated to specific wards."

Chapter 2

Gordon went on, "I work, as you know, on accidents and emergencies, which means that I see patients with injuries – such as unfortunate would-be kidnappers who have been shot in the hand by uncooperative victims – somewhat like Melpomene – as well as those who have ingested something that has disagreed with them, like sodium cyanide or bleach, which, you would hardly believe, is often stored in lemonade bottles. This means that I frequently seek advice from our extremely competent staff pharmacists. Most medical staff on general wards think this is beneath them and merely issue orders which are taken to the pharmacy service counter by nurses."

"So, if the ward doctor makes a mistake, it is only the vigilance of the dispensing pharmacist that can pick it up. Hence it is possible, especially at times of peak demand, for incorrect medications to be supplied to patients. It is unreasonable for nurses to check everything, and, frankly they are not knowledgeable enough – anyway, this is not their responsibility! Returning to the precipitated chalk incident, there is a further complication. That draught would have been prepared at the nurses' station, with powdered chalk from a jar measured into a glass and mixed with warm water from the tap. Each ward has such a station, with a medicine cabinet similar to what you might have at home, with common remedies such as precipitated chalk, flowers of sulphur, castor oil, syrup of figs, calamine lotion, Vaseline, aspirin tablets and so on – nothing more dangerous than those. It would be unnecessarily demanding of the pharmacy to make them responsible for day-to-day medicines and lotions."

"So, is it left to the nurses' discretion to administer these?" asked Melpomene.

"Not entirely. The ward doctor would make notes on a patient's chart sometimes, using the usual cabalistic abbreviations for dose and frequency that the nurses would understand – but, yes, much of this would be left to the ward sister or her nurses. And doctors would not be expected to bother about the appropriate treatment for, say, bed sores or constipation. These are plainly in the nurse's domain."

"So, it sounds as though our best starting point would be for us to go through your piles to get an overall feel for their contents," said Melpomene, "we will probably see relationships that might not have occurred to you, Gordon. Then maybe we can put our heads together in a day or two and decide on our next move. Before you go, though, I'd like to get your reaction to something."

"Go ahead with doing that, as you suggest, please, Mel – but what are you thinking of now?"

"It may be impractical, but I would like, if possible, to do some direct observation on the wards. Could I pretend to be, say, a nurses' aide, Gordon?"

"Sure, Melpomene, as long as you realise that your duties would include giving patients bed-pans, and then cleaning them up afterwards, as well as mopping up vomit and other rather distasteful activities – do you think you could cope? Of course, there would be other tasks too, that you might quite like!"

"I'll think about it!" said Mel, "maybe there are other ways of doing it!"

"If I think of any, I'll let you know when we meet again – when shall we do that, and where?"

It was decided that Gordon should come back to the agency in two days. As Alex said, "We don't want to show ourselves at your hospital unnecessarily in case we want to visit incognito at a later date to investigate particular issues. We should be able to scrutinise all your notes before we see you again and let you know whether they have given us a better idea of how to go ahead with our investigations."

They said goodbye to Gordon Salmon, and went back to sit in the office.

"Pity about the nurses' aide idea!" said Mel, "I rather like disguising myself and pretending to be someone I'm not, as you've probably noticed – but Gordon has put me right off with his talk of bed-pans!"

"You could go there as a policewoman, Mel, since you are officially a Special Constable and have all the uniform and equipment, but I can't think what your story would be – maybe we could save this up for later, once we have identified some villains and are ready to actually arrest someone! I've just had another thought – but let's fortify ourselves with tea and jam tarts first, and then I'll tell you about it."

They sat with the two secretaries to have their refreshments, and Marjorie said, "I really like the look of Doctor Salmon – he's the sort of doctor I'd want to look after me if I was in an accident or something. A lot of doctors seem to treat their patients as ignoramuses – or should that be ignorami? – but he seems to think that they are human beings."

"Now, now!" said Winnie, "I saw him first – just kidding, I'm sticking with my Tony for the moment! But Gordon may already be married or otherwise spoken for!"

"We'll discuss this later!" said the embarrassed Marjorie, with a blush beginning to suffuse her features.

"Changing the subject a little," said Alex, "what I remembered a few minutes ago was that I once used to go out with a medical student in her final year at University College Hospital – before you swept me off my feet, Mel! I've bumped into her a couple of times since and on the last occasion she told me she was specialising in infectious diseases and working as a consultant at UCH and another couple of hospitals in this general area. I'll give her a call; I should still have her number – only because I keep everybody's numbers, Mel! Perhaps she might have some bright ideas about how you could have access to the hospital in some role or other. I'll see if she can drop round to the flat for a drink or a meal tomorrow or some day soon – what do you think, Mel?"

"Good idea, my darling – then I can check her out and see whether I need to be worried about you!"

Mel and Alex started to go through Gordon's piles of notes. Melpomene started on the big pile that he hadn't said much about, except that they referred mainly to missing items, and after a few moments began sorting them into new piles, commenting, "I'm wondering if I can establish some relationships here, based on the person to whom the complaint was made in each case, and even try to apply the ideas of sociometry to them, so as not to waste everything I learnt from my degree in Social Anthropology. Then, if there actually are some groups, or gangs even, who are systematically robbing patients, this might start to show up. I'll give it a try, anyway – if nothing comes of it, this would be interesting too."

Chapter 3

This activity kept Melpomene and Alex busy until Winnie came and said, "Haven't you two got a home to go to? Marjorie and I are off, anyway – see you in the morning and don't forget to lock up!"

Alex asked, "What time is it? Probably too early to try to raise Vanessa Spring, my medical old flame, at her home, so I'll try later from the flat. I wonder what culinary delight Mrs Mountain is presenting us with tonight?"

"I think she was muttering about 'horso booko' as we left, so maybe we should pick up a bottle of red on the way home," said Mel, "I think we are nearly out of red, and I don't fancy drinking a white wine with such a substantial meal!"

The *osso bucco* indeed came up to Mrs M's usual standard, and since it was followed by bread-and-butter pudding, Mel and Alex were feeling more than replete as they pushed their chairs away from the table.

"I had better try to telephone Vanessa before I nod off!" said Alex, as he got out his precious note-book and thumbed through it to find her number.

The telephone was answered immediately, "Dr Spring here – I'm meant to be off duty tonight – is this an emergency?"

When Alex identified himself she relaxed immediately and they went into a long conversation of the 'long time no see', 'what have you been up to lately?' variety before Alex asked her, "Would you be free to come to dinner with us tomorrow? First to catch up, second to meet my wife, Melpomene, and third because we want to pick your brains about hospital procedures. Do these topics intrigue you enough? I should add that we have an excellent cook, capable of both traditional English and continental delicacies, so if you have a favourite dish that you have been missing lately, we can probably persuade Mrs Mountain to prepare it!"

When Vanessa replied, he said, "Excellent! I'll get that organised straight away! Would seven thirty suit you both? – fine, see you then!" and he gave the address.

Alex went to the kitchen to speak to Mrs M, "That meal was right up to your usual standards thanks very much! Would it be pushing you too much to ask you to cook beef Wellington for us and two guests tomorrow evening at 7.30? Followed by trifle? Wonderful!"

Mel had been listening and asked, "Two guests? Who is the second, then?"

"Vanessa's housemate, Imogen – I know no more about her than her name!"

The next morning at the office, Melpomene and Alex continued sorting through Gordon's notes. Mel was constructing a huge chart on a sheet of cartridge paper, showing small clusters of names and beginning to discover what might be connections between individuals and groups. She tried one of her notions out on Alex.

"See here, my love, in Gordon's pile there are eight complaints about missing cash – mostly small amounts. Four of these were made by patients in Nightingale Ward, and the names of the nurses on duty at the time seem to overlap. By the way, I think I'll ask Gordon if he can get hold of the duty rotas for all the wards for us, so we can see which nurses were on duty during which shifts. Anyway, the names Gillian and Hilda come up more than once in those four incidents. We shall have to encourage him to carry on making these notes – they look as though they could be very helpful."

"We shall have to be very careful, Mel, not to start making accusations, or even just jumping to conclusions – all these people are innocent until proved guilty, remember! Are there any names of people other than nurses who are mentioned?"

"I'll check! We can ask Gordon this sort of question when we see him tomorrow. I can already recall that a kid called Martin was directly accused of pinching change by one old dear – it appears that he is allowed to go round some of the wards selling evening newspapers. In fact, this kid could be a useful agent for us!"

"Like Sherlock Holmes' 'Baker Street Irregulars', eh, Mel?"

"Are you mocking me, Alex? – No, you would never do that, would you, my darling?"

"I'm going to take a break from all this sorting, Mel, and telephone Detective-Inspector Jimmy Manley, at Mile End Road station. I'd like to know whether there have been any more results from the Embassy case, and we haven't let Jimmy know about this job yet, either. He has been so helpful to us in the past, that it would be a pity not to keep in touch."

"You're right, Alex, and the same goes for our other useful contacts – but I don't think that this time it would take in the Foreign Office, or our continental network – this job is essentially local in scope. I might telephone some of the others, like Superintendent David Wilkinson in Woodhampton, as soon as you're done with Jimmy. But it must nearly be lunchtime, surely? Shall we go out to Guiseppe's trattoria, or get the girls to fetch us something?"

"Let's ask Winnie – she'll want something for herself, anyway. Marjorie usually has something packed for her by her Mum. I'll ring Jimmy now – I have his number permanently engraved on my brain."

He spoke to Jimmy Manley for several minutes and then thanked him and rang off, telling Mel that Jimmy had said that he would ask the boys at Finchley North station whether they had had any official complaints from the hospital and that trial dates had been set for several of the villains from the Embassy case, and that Alex and Mel would receive summons in due course for those where they were required to appear as witnesses.

"I shall enjoy that!" said Mel, "It will be nice to see some of them squirm, particularly the one I had to shoot!"

"I hope you are not being vindictive, Mel – that's not like you at all!"

"All very well, for you, Alex, you didn't have a pistol shoved in the back of your neck while you were wondering whether you would be dead soon! I only want to see him get the punishment he deserves! A bullet in the hand doesn't cover it, in my opinion!"

In the event, Mel and Alex went to Guiseppe's for a lightish meal, *pizza quattro stagioni*, given that they had to leave room for the Beef Wellington at dinner time. Then they did some more sorting, said goodbye to Marjorie and Winnie, and went home.

Chapter 4

Caroline showed their guests in promptly at half-past seven. Vanessa embraced Alex warmly – but not too warmly, Melpomene thought – and introduced herself to Mel.

She was a little taller than Mel, but not so tall as to be distinctive for a woman, with her brown hair in a shingle bob. She drew her friend forward, saying, "This is Imogen, who is my good friend and sometimes my assistant – she is a postgraduate student at University College, studying bacteriology. And before you start speculating – no, we are not emotionally involved!"

Imogen, a rather stocky woman with long fair hair gathered in a bun, smiled at this – she was apparently accustomed to people drawing inferences – and said, "Vanessa and I have a research project going on the ways that infections spread in hospitals, so when I'm not in the lab I collect swabs around the wards."

"That's very interesting!" said Melpomene, "I'll talk to you later about that, Imogen. Now come in and have an apéritif before dinner – we have Dubonnet if you like that, and two sorts of vermouth, too."

Over the drinks, and the courses that followed, a variety of topics were discussed. Imogen was particularly interested in finding out about the ways that detectives went about their work. When Alex and Mel explained, and described how they approached a couple of their previous cases, Imogen said, "That sounds quite similar to scientific research – forming hypotheses, gathering facts to test them and coming to conclusions – that is very like what Vanessa and I are doing!"

"I am actually a social scientist myself," said Mel, "my degree from LSE is in Social Anthropology, a discipline that takes a rather similar approach. What I should like to know, Imogen, do you collect any of your data from Finchley Hospital? I'm wondering whether I could pretend to act as your assistant, say, which will give me a cover story while I gather my own evidence about possible illicit activities that we are looking into there for Gordon Salmon – perhaps you or Vanessa know him?"

"Only vaguely," Vanessa replied, "He's in accident and emergency, isn't he? There's not much connection between that and infectious diseases, so our paths don't tend to cross."

Imogen said, "Getting back to your question, Melpomene – yes, I quite often do the rounds at Finchley, not only the medical wards but also some of the others, because we are interested in the general spread of bacteria. You could carry the case with my instruments and collecting phials for me, Mel, which would be a great help, actually. Have you got a white coat? If not I can easily lend you one of mine, though you might have to belt it up tightly to fit your sylph-like figure!"

"That sounds very promising, Imogen – when are you due to visit Finchley next? Can I also wear one of those little white caps to cover my blonde curls – apparently they are my most attractive and distinctive feature – according to Alex anyway!"

Alex suggested that they stop talking shop, and kicked off by asking Vanessa what she did as relaxation and as a change from work.

"Good question, Alex – in fact Imogen and I share two rather athletic pursuits – squash racquets and fencing. As it happens, we met through the latter sport – we were drawn as opponents in a fairly low division of the University fencing championships – I beat her by a small margin on that occasion, but I think honours are about even by now!"

"But there is no doubt about Vanessa's prowess at squash!" said Imogen, "I am just not as nimble as her around the court, so she beats me eight games out of ten. And apart from sport, I write short stories for women's magazines – you know – 'at one bound he was by her side' and 'he crushed her to his manly chest and she nearly swooned' – that sort of thing! I've actually had some published – the weeklies have a constant need to fill their pages with more than knitting tips and menu suggestions!"

The evening passed in these pleasant ways until Vanessa said, "Look at the time! If I don't get in my seven hours I will be useless tomorrow, and Imogen and I have the lab at University College booked for the day. Thank you for a lovely evening, Mel and Alex, we must return the compliment soon – but it will have to be at a restaurant – we haven't got a super cook like you two!"

"And we'll negotiate a time and arrangements for our expedition into darkest Finchley Hospital," said Imogen, "I've got your home and work numbers, Mel – I'm looking forward to it!"

When the guests had put on their warm coats and scarves Melpomene and Alex walked them down to the street, Alex asking, "Did you come by tube? I could run you home if you want – I don't know how frequently they run at this time of night."

"Oh, no problem!" said Imogen, "Here is our carriage! – it's the latest Brough Superior!" as she indicated a motor-cycle combination parked close by. She unlocked a pannier-bag and took out two flying helmets with pairs of goggles attached, while Vanessa seated herself in the sidecar. Then she leapt on the kick-starter and the huge engine burst into life. The two women waved happily to Alex and Mel, who were still standing, somewhat shocked, as they shot off up the street.

In fact, Mel was more entranced than shocked, with her eyes shining, so Alex said forcefully. "No, Mel, no! We are definitely not getting a motorcycle!"

Melpomene may have dreamed of motorcycles that night, but still awoke at her customary hour the next day and tackled her usual substantial breakfast.

They drove to the office and had a discussion over tea and jam tarts before Gordon Salmon turned up as arranged. Melpomene told him of her plans to become a research assistant, and after thinking a few moments, he nodded and said, "Yes, I think that will work. You can have a notepad, and anyone who sees you making notes will assume that they are about your tests. I believe I saw your friend talking to the sister in charge of one of the wards a little while ago. Is she a hefty blonde lady?"

"Well, yes, but I think she would prefer to be called something different from hefty!"

"Right," said Alex, "let us see how that works out once Mel has had a few hours on the job. Meanwhile, I'd like to talk about a few things we've noticed about your notes, Gordon."

Then they started turning over the new arrangements of piles and adding to Melpomene's chart, which impressed Gordon, "It starts to make sense when you can see how these topics are interrelated," he said, "I believe I did right in coming to you!"

Chapter 5

After a couple of hours, Gordon Salmon looked at his watch and said, "I ought to be getting back to the hospital – I've left a young houseman in charge of A and E, and I don't want him to be overstressed if something unusual comes up. Let me know if and when you need me for the next step. Will you be doing your rounds with Imogen soon, Mel?"

"I'll need to telephone her at home this evening, Gordon," said Mel, "she and Vanessa are doing lab work at UC all day today. By the way, if I see you at the hospital in the future, at any stage, I shall purposely ignore you, so please don't take offence!"

When Gordon had gone, Alex said that he would try Jimmy again, to see whether his North Finchley colleagues had anything to report about complaints about thefts from hospital patients.

Jimmy replied, "Nothing exactly like that, Alex, but they did have a call from the matron, asking them if they could do anything about a homeless eccentric, called 'Smoky Joe' by the locals, who has been coming into the wards and bothering patients by asking for change. One elderly lady, with a broken leg that had just been plastered, was quite frightened when he shook her to wake her up. The station sent an officer to speak with the matron, but he had to point out to her that there are doormen at the main and ambulance entrances, so it was up to them to send the man away – the police could do nothing unless the hospital wished to prefer a specific charge. I only mention this because it is possible that this benighted soul is doing a bit of pilfering as well as begging."

"Thanks, Jimmy – sorry to bother you over such trivialities! Any more repercussions from our last case?"

"I think we are going to have quite a fight over the former embassy military attaché, Alex. He has engaged a high-profile barrister, who has already made an application for bail, which I'm glad to say was rejected by the judge who heard it, on the grounds both of the seriousness of the offence and Brigadier Douglas' risk of flight! Oh, that reminds me, I keep meaning to tell you that the Guernsey police have picked up Henri Mercier and his companion, who were spotted fleeing Calais by speedboat when Commissaire Principal Hugo Palance and his Sûreté men rounded up their gang of rum-runners, so your efforts have borne fruit both sides of the Channel!"

As Alex hung up the telephone and turned to go back to his place, he saw a pile of brochures and advertisements, the top one of which caught his eye. It was headed, 'Hathaway and Woodruff – Wholesale Distributors of Cleaning Materials and Bulk Pharmaceuticals' "Where is this from, Marjorie?" he asked.

"Oh we get lots of those, some in the mail and some put through the door," she said, "I keep some of them, because Mrs Wilson, the office cleaner, asks me to get various things when she is running low – floor polish, bleach, methylated spirits for the windows and so on. They're much cheaper from the wholesalers than from the High Street shops – of course, they come in larger sizes, but that's no problem."

"I didn't even know we had an office cleaner!" said Alex, "Well, you didn't imagine that Winnie and I got down on our hands and knees, did you? You've never seen her because she comes very early, when you're still in your beddy-byes!"

"I shall give these people a call," said Alex, "this has sent my mind off on another tack!"

A woman answered the phone and Alex said, "I have an enquiry about pharmaceuticals – who would be the best person there to talk to?" She replied, "I'll transfer you to Mr David Woodruff – fortunately you have caught him in the office, unless he has already gone to lunch."

"Woodruff here," said a voice, "how can I help?"

"First," said Alex, "do you deal directly with hospitals?"

"Oh yes, we supply University College Hospital, King's College, Guy's and two or three others."

"How about Finchley General? I have a contact there."

"Not yet," replied Woodruff, "but I'm going there in a day or two. I believe that their current supplier is giving trouble."

"How would you feel about getting together with me over drinks, this afternoon, at somewhere convenient for you? My name is Alan Robertson and I think we might be able to do business!"

"Certainly!" said Woodruff eagerly, "how about the Goat and Compasses Grill, in Bayswater Road? They know me there, so you can ask for me by name. Shall we say 4.30?"

When Alex rang off, Melpomene asked, "What was that all about, Mr Robertson?"

Alex passed her the brochure, "The idea is this, Mel – it's not guaranteed to work, of course, but what I'm going to do is to try to convince this lot, Hathaway and Woodruff, that I have some connection with the procurements officer – or whatever they call him or her – at the hospital. Then I shall pump enough information out of David Woodruff over drinks this afternoon so that I can, in turn, convince the hospital people that I am somehow acting for him. All this is simply so that I have an excuse for asking questions to find out how the hospital pharmacy operates. I shall not, of course, actually make any deals!"

"You realize, my darling, that once you've spoken to these people you will have blown any cover you might once have had! This means that you will effectively be hors de combat from then onward!"

"But what I haven't explained, Mel, is that it is only over the drinks with Woodruff that I shall be face to face. All the hospital conversations will be conducted over the telephone!"

Melpomene looked dubious, "Best of luck, Alex, it seems to me that that would be like playing bridge in the dark! I suppose that a skilful barrister might be able to keep all the balls in the air at once – but you are merely a humble solicitor."

"I did come out top in Moot Court at University two terms running, so I hope some of those skills are still with me. We shall see, shall we not! I'd better go now else I shall be late at the Goat and Compasses. See you at home, where I shall crow over my success, or weep over my ignominious failure!"

"I shall prepare myself for either eventuality, Alex – go and break a leg!"

Melpomene consoled herself with a fresh pot of Lapsang Souchong, but she still felt rather anxious. Then she drained her cup, squared her shoulders, said goodbye to Marjorie and Winnie and set off home. Alex had taken the Riley, so she decided to walk, as it would only take fifteen minutes, and she felt she needed the exercise.

Chapter 6

Alex parked on Bayswater Road not far from the restaurant and strolled up to the front door. Inside, a waiter approached him and he said, "I'm joining Mr Woodruff, could you point him out for me, please?"

He was taken to a corner table, where Woodruff stood up and shook his hand. He was well-dressed, even a touch flashy, with carefully slicked-down black hair. Alex thought to himself, "I'll bet he's worked his way up in the firm from being a sales rep!"

"Shall we start with a drink?" said Woodruff, who was already nursing what looked like a cocktail. "Just a white wine, thanks, I'm driving!" said Alex, "I'll get straight to the point – the people at Finchley Hospital are looking around for alternative suppliers, as they are having a few problems. Nothing major, you understand, just an occasional awkwardness – I gather there have been one or two misunderstandings in the past. I am merely acting as an intermediary – I have no direct connection with the hospital."

"I see," said Woodruff, "I can quite understand – if I'm right, their present suppliers are Katzenberg Ethicals, for controlled drugs, Hardcastle Brothers, for general pharmaceuticals, and Simpson and Drury for cleaning products and antiseptics. I looked these up after I spoke with you on the telephone – we in the trade make it our business to keep an eye on our competitors, you see! With what particular area are your clients having difficulties? Let's order, shall we? I can recommend the Dover sole here, or you might prefer a meat dish."

"The sole sounds good to me!" said Alex, "As for difficulties, the hospital has no problem with the housekeeping side of things, more in the medicine areas. What is your firm's coverage there?"

"We can certainly cover Hardcastle's range, but we don't really venture into all the controlled drugs – we can supply most opiates, but we have no source for cocaine and the like. What if you ask your people – the head pharmacist preferably – to put together a trial shopping list, then I can indicate to them what we can supply and what we will have to source elsewhere, without commitment, of course!"

They chatted some more until Alex thanked him, shook hands and left. As he was walking back to the car he realized he could have asked Woodruff to tell him who would be the best person at Finchley Hospital to talk to, but on second thoughts he decided that this might have sounded suspicious, since he had claimed he was already in contact. He would certainly have to keep his wits about him!

Back at the flat, Melpomene was talking to Mrs Mountain, telling her that Alex might be running late. "He was going to have a meal with a client, so I'm not sure whether he will be ready for one of your splendid dinners yet – maybe we could have it a bit later than usual – are you cooking something that can be delayed?"

"As it happens, ma'am, I'm giving you poached carp, so I only have to put it on for about twenty minutes – and the salad ain't no bother, neither. And for afters we've got a strawberry blermonge mould. Would eight o'clock be all right?"

Alex arrived just after this conversation and gratefully accepted a cup of tea, over which he related his meeting with Woodruff, saying that he had extracted enough information from him to put together a convincing story for the hospital on the next day.

"I had a call from Imogen just now," said Mel, "they had a profitable day in the lab – Vanessa and she are submitting an article to a journal of microbiology and the results from today's tests will finish it off. So Imogen suggests that we have our first tour of the wards tomorrow, when she will show me what she does and introduce me to some key people, like Matron and the sisters in charge of various wards. After that, I should be able to poke about without attracting undue attention. I shall be calling myself Henrietta Musgrave again."

"My head is buzzing with plans for tomorrow," said Alex, "so I think I had better carry on reading the latest Hercule Poirot novel by Agatha Christie, 'The Murder of Roger Ackroyd', that I got from the library the other day on Winnie's recommendation."

"And I shall do the cryptic crosswords from the last two days' papers – I'm dropping badly behind!" said Melpomene, "another cup?"

They were just finishing breakfast the next morning when the doorbell rang, to disclose Imogen, who handed Mel a flying-

17

helmet and goggles and said, "Wrap up well – it's a wee bit parky this morning – I've got the sidecar seat full of my gear, so it's the pillion for you I'm afraid."

"I shan't mind!" said Mel, "In fact, can we go the long way round to the hospital? I'm looking forward to my first motor-cycle ride since I was in second year at LSE and had a mad boyfriend who used to let me drive sometimes! But I'm not prepared to attempt a combination, yet – don't worry!"

So, after an exhilarating – for Mel – twenty-minute drive, Imogen parked near the ambulance entrance of the hospital, showed Mel how to put the helmets safely away in the lockable panniers and took her to the matron's office, each carrying a case of equipment.

Melpomene had expected the matron to be a traditional authority figure, even a harridan, but in reality Matron Stevenson was a pleasant, slightly plump woman who greeted her warmly as Imogen introduced her as "My friend and colleague Henrietta Musgrave, who is going to give me a hand with our survey. Vanessa Spring sends her regards, by the way."

"I'm sure you will get on well together! You will show Mrs Musgrave where you can leave your coats and change into your overalls, Miss Preston, won't you? If you need me for anything, you know where to come."

Imogen showed Melpomene to a cloakroom, and opened a locker "They've given me my own locker and key, so we can store our stuff safely. I've brought you a white coat – see how it fits – it really doesn't matter if it's a bit loose."

Mel said, "Matron seems very nice – I was expecting someone a lot more rigid – I suppose I read too many hospital romances when I was a lot younger. But she is no slouch, she spotted my wedding ring straight away!"

"Don't be deceived, Mel – she can assert herself when she feels it necessary – I've seen young nurses brought to tears when she caught them slacking or making a mistake. But you should be safe, at least for a while! Come and see my first subject, and I'll show you what we do. Please bring the brown case and I'll take the black one – we'll go to McTavish ward first and I'll introduce you to the ward supervisor, Sister Wood – now she really can be a termagant sometimes, so be careful!"

Chapter 7

Melpomene was introduced to Sister Wood, who was courteous, if a little distant. Imogen asked her which patients on McTavish Ward she could see and take swabs from, and which she should avoid.

"I anticipated your request, Miss Preston, so I got one of our probationers to list all the names and bed numbers. I have been through it and marked it up – ticks for those you may test and crosses for those you should not disturb. Of course, you know my requirements and precautions – please make sure Mrs Musgrave understands these directives and follows them. I imagine you will need no more than an hour or two to complete your rounds – of course if you find that a patient is being attended to by a nurse, you should skip him or her for a while. Please do the males first and make sure that the doors of that section are closed when you leave – some of them try to sneak peeks at the women if they are not watched! Off you go!"

Imogen and Melpomene went to the first man on Sister's list. Imogen greeted him by name and explained who they were and that they were doing "an important University research project on how germs spread" and that all they would just rub a cotton bud on the inside of his cheek, "It won't hurt – you'll hardly notice!"

She took a new swab in a closed tube from the supply in Melpomene's case, did the swabbing on the man's cheek and sealed it up in the tube again, wrote the date and patient's name on the label, and then put it away in her own case. "Thank you very much!" she said to the man, who asked "Are you going to make a report on this? I'm in here for stomach pains, what's that got to do with my cheek?"

"Oh, you are right to ask! What we're trying to find out is whether you have any germs in your system that might be causing your stomach ache!" she said, "The results will be published in a medical journal, but not for a while, I'm afraid!"

This procedure was repeated for all the other men ticked on the list, with similar results, and then they left the men's section of the ward, Imogen saying, "Would you like to try that yourself with some of the women patients while I watch?"

Melpomene said she would, of course, and proceeded to test half a dozen women. Imogen was impressed and said "I hope you don't think this was a waste of time, even though you are really here for another purpose. I would guess that you now feel more confident in talking with patients, so you can now chat with them and see whether you can come up with any information that might be valuable for your investigation.

"I'll try something with the next one, Imogen, and you must tell me whether you think it is acceptable."

So, at the next bed, as soon as she had taken the swab and told the woman the purpose of the test, she went on, in a conversational tone, "How are you finding it here – I know it's never very pleasant being in a hospital, but are the staff treating you well? No problems with the doctors or nurses or the arrangements here?"

This brought an immediate result – the woman said, in an annoyed middle-class voice, "Well I am glad somebody cares! I've been trying to tell them for days now, but all they say is 'dear, dear' or something, and I just know nothing will be done! The problem is that people are taking things from my locker while I'm asleep! I brought in about four novels – just fairly trashy ones, like Ethel M Dell or Elinor Glyn – because I thought I would have time to read while I was in here – fat chance, actually, because they're always wanting to take my temperature or do another test or give me a blanket bath or something – don't take offence, dear, I'm not talking about you! Anyway, I only have two books left now! Besides the books, I've lost a bottle of eau de cologne – I'm sure I brought one in, because it's good for headaches – and a lipstick that I wanted to put on yesterday when my dear husband came to visit – that's missing, too! I don't like to accuse anyone of course, but I believe it's the women who mop the floors and so on."

Melpomene said, "I can't promise anything, but if I get a chance I'll make some enquiries for you. Are you here for long?"

"They say another week, but I don't think they really know – the specialist who came in and examined me said I had neurasthenia – but I just think I've been working too hard – I have a little gift shop, you know."

Mel and Imogen went round taking swabs from the other women in the ward, and Melpomene asked each one how she was finding the hospital, but most of them had no complaints until they reached the last patient ticked on Sister Wood's list.

She was an immensely overweight woman, and once Mel had swabbed her cheek, she opened up with a tirade of abuse, "I'm surprised you've got the nerve to ask me that – if I could get up I'd have the p'leece on the lot of 'em – they ain't feeding me right and they've even took me biscuits and choc'lates off of me as soon as I was in me bed. And that one with the fancy 'at, she's the worst of the lot – I reckon she's trying to poison me! I'm s'posed to have me stummick tablets every two hours, but that one's been trying make me to swaller some 'orrible med'cine – and when I said I wouldn't she got two of her nurses to hold me arms while she pinched me nose and forced it down me!"

Imogen tried to placate her by saying that she would speak to somebody, but by then the woman was getting red in the face and shaking, so all Mel and Imogen could do was to steal away to the ward office and speak to Sister Wood.

"Mrs Woodcock is a bit of a problem isn't she?" said Imogen, "How do you cope with patients like that?" Sister answered, "Yes, it's very difficult, but next time she has something to eat and drink – which won't be long, she's very greedy – she'll get a little something extra which should settle her down!"

"Will you have to do that with every meal?" asked Mel, "Yes, but she'll be discharged in a day or two – there's really no evidence of any disease, so we won't need to keep her."

As they went to put their white coats away and collect their warm clothes and scarves for the ride home, Melpomene said, "That was a very valuable exercise for me, Imogen – when can we do another ward?"

"Not tomorrow, because Vanessa and I have to prepare plates from today's swabs for microscopic examination, by growing cultures on an agar medium in Petri dishes – how about the day after?"

"That sounds fine – but meanwhile I'm getting quite interested in all this – could I come to your lab some time and see how it's all done?"

"Come tomorrow if you like – I can pick you up with the Brough about nine o'clock, if that suits you."

21

Chapter 8

Then Melpomene said "I don't know about you, Imogen, but I'm famished! Let's go and get a late lunch somewhere, unless you have other plans – my treat!"

Imogen didn't have other suggestions, so they found a little Lebanese restaurant and had mezze, with tabouleh, hummus, baba ghanoush, kebbeh and stuffed grape leaves – which were all new to Imogen, "But I shall certainly remember these dishes for the future – thank you Mel!"

Melpomene was dropped off at home, and Alex returned to the flat an hour later. They exchanged accounts of their day's activities, Mel first, and then Alex told how he had telephoned the hospital switch and asked to speak to the procurement officer.

"The operator didn't quite know what I meant – they don't use that term in the hospital – but after a little more explanation from me, she put me onto the Chief Pharmacist, who was very helpful. Her name is Elspeth McCracken, and she is responsible for making lists of orders for drugs and medicines required for the pharmacy, but not for the actual purchasing, which is done by someone working under the Director of Finance. So I asked Elspeth whether that person would also look after other hospital supplies, and she said she thought so, but maybe I should speak to him directly. His name is Henry Jackson and she told me his telephone number."

"Did you tell her why you were interested, Alex?"

"I just said I was speaking for an interested party, and this prompted her to say that she hoped it was nobody at Hardcastle's, because she was getting fed up with constant mix-ups in their service – wrong products, wrong quantities and that sort of thing. This made me prick up my ears of course, Mel!"

"What did Mr Jackson have to say?"

"He wasn't there! Somebody else asked if they could help, but I thanked her and said I would try Jackson later – she said he was out talking to suppliers and would probably be in tomorrow morning. This gave me an idea, so I got Winnie to

22

look up the number for Hardcastle Brothers and make a call – avoiding telling them it was from a firm of investigators!"

"I told her I wouldn't speak myself, because I was getting a bit suspicious of Jackson and didn't want to risk my voice being recognized later, so asked her to say that she was trying to contact Mr Jackson, from Finchley Hospital, on a matter of some urgency, and that she understood that he might be at their depot talking to one of their pharmaceutical representatives and would it be possible to find him for her?"

"I was listening on the second earpiece, of course, so when I heard a man answer, and say he was Jackson, I passed Winnie a note that I had just scribbled, which said something like *'I'm speaking for Mr Alan Robertson, who has interests at your hospital and would like to talk to you, preferably somewhere other than at the hospital.'* "

"Winnie is quick on the uptake, so she recited this script very convincingly, and then went on to answer him *ad lib*, saying that a café would seem to be ideal, and did he have a particular one in mind?"

"He told her a name and location and asked whether two-thirty would be suitable. I gave Winnie the nod, so she told him it would! At the arranged time, I drove to the address he had given and parked. Then I saw someone standing outside and clearly waiting for someone, so I went up, asked whether he was Mr Jackson and introduced myself."

Melpomene was becoming very interested, "So what happened? Did you get anything interesting from this man?"

"Be patient, my darling and I will reveal all! As one does, I had visualised Jackson, and as often happens, I was dead wrong! He would have been perfect casting for the rural Dean in a drawing-room comedy! I need not describe him further, but will point out that I was not deceived by that innocent exterior."

"We found a quiet table and ordered coffee and pastries. Then, of course, he asked me what this was all about. So I told him that I had been given the impression that Hardcastle's was unreliable, or even shifty! I was keeping a close watch on his changing expressions as I said this, while trying not to appear too interested – and when I uttered the word 'shifty', his eyes dilated and his mouth tightened! I tried not to react to this and went on to say that there appeared to be very little hard evidence of anything untoward – at which he seemed to relax."

"Dis you explain your interest in the hospital, Alex? Had I been in Jackson's shoes, that would have intrigued me, at the very least!"

"I decided to proceed on the principle that I would tell him things that he could find out easily, while keeping other matters close to my chest, so I said that I had been talking to Elspeth McCracken and that she was bothered by the service she was getting from Hardcastle's – frequent errors in deliveries, both wrong products and wrong quantities, and that she had told me that he was the person dealing with suppliers, while she simply made out the shopping lists."

"He said that, indeed, he was the one who located suppliers, negotiated prices and placed orders, not only for consumable supplies but also for linen and hardware – including bed-pans and glassware. This meant that he was often out of the hospital, visiting firms in the London area but also elsewhere, like the Midlands and the North."

"Then I asked him what would happen if a supplier – Hardcastle's for example – had problems, such as late deliveries, defective merchandise, missed orders and so on. Was it he who sorted out these difficulties – and how much discretion did he have?"

"He appeared to puff himself up a little and told me that he had the confidence of the Board and the hospital management, who left him to make all the important decisions!"

"So," said Melpomene, "unless this man truly has the ethical character of a rural Dean, as well as the appearance of one, he is in a position to make a very nice income for himself on the side! He could stand over the suppliers and demand inducements, threatening that he would withdraw their contracts if they failed to treat him right!"

"We must both have developed a degree of cynicism, my love, because that is exactly the way that I was thinking. But, we are now obliged to discover hard evidence – we cannot proceed on the basis of conjecture alone."

Mel agreed, "Gordon Salmon has started to amass a body of anecdotal material – what we need now is indisputable fact to support this. And we have already started!"

Chapter 9

Over dinner that evening, Melpomene realized she hadn't told Alex what she would be doing the next day.

"I'm going to University College with Imogen to see how she runs tests on the swabs we took. This will be interesting in its own right, but it may also give me a chance to make further enquiries about supplies. The microbiology lab must buy in a variety of different materials for its work, so I'll see if any of them come from the firms we're already looking into."

"And I shall go to talk with Elspeth McCracken, since she mentioned the problems she was having with suppliers," said Alex, "I know I said that I would do everything over the telephone, but I believe that Elspeth is too valuable a contact for that. I'll try to be as discreet as possible – anyway Henry Jackson already knows I've spoken to her. I'll take something that could look like a sample case with me, so that if I'm spotted by anyone else they will only take me for a rep. What do you think?"

"Put plenty of this new Brylcreem hair dressing on and they will be in no doubt of that! Should you wear that double-breasted beige suit of yours that I hate, to complete the picture?"

"Leave it to me, my pet, I'm only sorry I haven't got time to develop a suitable Adolphe Menjou moustache!"

After breakfast the next day, Imogen arrived with the Brough to go to the lab, Mel once again taking the pillion seat, since the precious sample cases were travelling in the sidecar.

"I'm afraid we shall have a bit of a walk across the University grounds," said Imogen, "they're getting a bit particular about parking inside these days – even some undergraduates have cars now."

On the way to the Microbiology building, each carrying a case, they passed a windowless building with two vans backed up to a loading dock. Mel asked what it was, and Imogen said she didn't really know, but it might be the main University store. "I've seen trollies loaded with cardboard boxes being wheeled into our building by a porter in a brown overall, so there must be a central warehouse somewhere about."

Melpomene said, "Excuse me a moment – can I leave this case with you? I just want to look at these vans."

She walked back and saw that a driver was getting into one of the vans. She addressed him, saying, "Excuse me please, if you don't mind, can you tell me what you were just delivering?"

"That's all right, missus, I were just dropping off some boxes of chemicals – I suppose that's what they are, seeing they're from Simpson and Drury's. I just deliver 'em – it's no business of mine what's in the boxes! Now I've got to get back on me rounds, I've got lots of other stuff to deliver!"

He tipped his cap, started his van and drove off. Mel saw that the second van was unattended, but that there was a name on the side – 'Willoughby's Stationery Supplies'.

She hurried back to Imogen and said, "Sorry for the delay – I didn't find out much anyway!" Then she picked up her case and followed Imogen to the Microbiology department, which looked pretty modern, in contrast to the other University buildings, some of which were even covered with the traditional ivy.

Inside, the sense of modernity persisted – there were long brightly-lit corridors lined with windows through which laboratories or lecture rooms full of students could be seen. Imogen opened a door and ushered Mel into a small laboratory with three benches littered with apparatus of various kinds. There was a group of students by one of them surrounding a demonstrator who was explaining patiently what they would soon be seeing through a microscope. As he spotted Imogen he gave a cheery wave, saying, "You don't feel like taking over here, do you? One of my previous class said he couldn't see anything, and I had to show him how to take the lens cap off!"

"Sorry, Clem, I've got a lot of my own stuff to attend to today – maybe another time." She put the two cases down by an empty bench and said, "I've got a couple of racks of Petri dishes with Agar medium sterilizing in an autoclave, over here. It's on a timer – I popped in early this morning to set it up before I came for you, Mel. Put some clean cotton gloves on, and please don't open any of these till I show you what to do."

Over the next hour or so, she showed Melpomene how to transfer what was on the swabs to the jelly-like medium, taking precautions not to contaminate it by touching the sides or anything else, and labelling the lids for identification.

"What we shall do next, Mel," she said, "is put all the Petri dishes in a nice warm cabinet for an incubation period, so that any bacteria can grow nicely if they want to. If they do, we will be able to see that colonies have developed on the Agar, and then we can transfer these to microscope slides for examination. Only then will we find out what we've captured! I'll let you know the results then, of course! If a paper comes of this, I'll list you as a co-author!"

There being nothing more that could be done, Imogen ran Melpomene home again.

"That was fascinating, Imogen, thank you very much! Will you come in for a cup of tea or something?"

"I won't say no, I wouldn't mind a bun or whatever, either – it's been a long time since my breakfast – I got up at the break of dawn to sterilise those Petri dishes!"

"I'll see what Mrs M can conjure up!" said Mel, "I'm somewhat peckish myself – Alex says I'm perpetually that way, and I must admit he's not really wrong!"

Mrs Mountain was reliable as usual, and soon presented the pair with what she called country omelettes, with Worcestershire sauce, cheese and spring onions, and served with fried potatoes.

After that they were both settling down with cups of Lapsang Souchong when Alex arrived. He sniffed the air, saying, "Something smells delicious – what a pity I have just had a hospital lunch with Elspeth McCracken in the staff common-room. I was originally going to sample the main cafeteria, but she discouraged me, telling me it would be a disappointment for anyone with a sophisticated palate!"

"Apart from lunch with the no-doubt charming Elspeth," said Melpomene, "did you gain anything from your visit?"

"Oh, yes! But as well as cementing a friendship, I think I've also made an enemy! I was in Elspeth's office when she had an unexpected visitor, who was more than somewhat put out when he saw me with her!"

"Do you mean he was a jealous rival for her affections, Alex? Or what? Do tell us!"

Chapter 10

"It was our rural dean look-alike, Henry Jackson," said Alex, "and his first piqued remark when he saw me there was to the effect that it looked as though I was checking up on him! Of course I mollified him by saying that I had told him when I met him earlier that I was keeping in touch with Elspeth, but my overwhelming impression was that he was somebody with a guilty conscience! We shall have to watch dear Mr Jackson closely – while being careful not to feed his suspicions any further."

"Maybe you should pass the ball to me, since he is unaware of our relationship," said Melpomene, "but I shall have to contrive a good excuse to speak to him – I'll see what I can come up with. Anyway, what happened with Elspeth – did you find out anything new that could be interesting to us?"

"Actually I did, Mel, but it was something that happened over lunch. As I said, we were having it in the staff common-room, and as we walked in, who should I spy at a corner table, with his back to us, fortunately, but the self-same cleric, our Dean Jackson, engaged in conversation with a little bald man in a brown suit with, would you believe, an Adolphe Menjou moustache. I had to stop myself laughing out loud, given our recent conversation! I tried not to look at the pair too obviously, but I did notice a briefcase next to Adolphe's chair."

"When Elspeth and I had found a table on the other side of the room and ordered, I asked her, quite casually, if she knew the man with Jackson. She looked at me very hard and whispered, 'Yes – he is a Mr Dodson, from one of our suppliers – Katzenberg's – I had an argument with him only last week! I had opened one of his firm's cartons that was labelled milk of magnesia, only to find that it contained a potassium bromide preparation instead. Now the bottles were clearly labelled, so there was not much chance of mistakes, but, as I said to him when he came in to replace the carton, if a patient had been given a largish dose, then instead of settling the stomach as intended, it might have induced nausea and even vomiting!' I could see that Elspeth was still quite upset over this incident!"

There then ensued a long discussion about their next moves. Melpomene said she would continue helping Imogen to take swabs, whenever she was at Finchley again, since in other wards there might be more patients with complaints about pilfering and questionable medication.

As she said, "We know in which wards Gordon Salmon found incidents worth noting, but he never claimed to cover the ground exhaustively, and in any case the population of patients is constantly changing, so I'm not worried about duplication. I must have another sort through Gordon's notes – my view might have shifted in the meantime, after visiting the hospital myself. And it sounds, Alex, that you have more than one lead to follow up. Would it be worthwhile asking Jimmy Manley whether any of our suspects rings a bell for him?"

"Why not – if they don't, they don't, and no harm done. By the way, Mel, did you get round to asking Gordon whether he could get copies of the ward duty rotas for us? He mentions several of the nurses' names in his notes, so it would be interesting to see whether they might have been on duty when other things happened, as well as those that were directly involved in them. Did you encounter many nurses while you were collecting swabs?"

"Sister Wood is the only one whose name I know – there were other nurses around, of course – we had to bypass a few patients who were being attended to – but I was so intent on the swab business that I never thought to look at their name tags – *mea culpa, mea maxima culpa!* But, now I think of it, I saw some other women wearing green overalls, and I asked Imogen whether they were nurses' aides or what. You may recall I proposed masquerading as one of those myself – until Gordon told me about bed-pans!"

"And were you right, Mel?"

"No – apparently nurses' aides at Finchley Hospital wear pink overalls – the green ones are women from the catering service – they take meals on trays to the bed-ridden patients. We had better find out about them, too – if they are in and out of the wards they might have as much opportunity to pilfer things as anyone else – not that I have any definite suspicions, of course."

Alex was pondering further, "So, all in all, there are several lots of people going in and out of the wards, Mel – doctors, nurses, nurses' aides, catering staff, and professional people like physiotherapists and audiologists, as well as social workers, I suppose."

"And private detectives, too, Alex, some of them pretending to be research assistants! And the occasional policeman, I should think – and paper boys!"

"It's a pity you've already identified yourself as a researcher's assistant, Mel, otherwise you might have been able to get a job as a lunch lady! We ought to find out whether they are hospital employees or work for an outside catering firm – I might telephone Henry Jackson, he would know. I still have his number, I think."

While Alex was telephoning, Melpomene chatted some more with Imogen, who said she didn't know much about the caterers either, except that she had seen the same green-clad women at University College Hospital too, so it was possible that they were provided by an outside company.

"I shall be at UCH tomorrow, Mel, so I could ask the management there about them if you like – and this will avoid drawing the attention of people at Finchley, too."

"My word, Imogen, I do believe you are beginning to acquire some of the devious characteristics of a private investigator! Good thinking – please see what you can find out for us."

Alex finished his telephoning and said that, once again, the rural Dean was away from his desk – possibly visiting his flock. When Mel told him Imogen's idea, he agreed they could hold off until they found out what she could learn about the caterers.

"Let's not build up our expectations, though – they are very likely decent folk, free from sin – of the kind we are looking for, anyway!"

"Have you two emptied the tea-pot? I'm about ready for a cup now – any jam tarts or cake? It's a long time until dinner – is Imogen staying to join us for a meal?"

"Much as I would like that, Alex," relied Imogen, "I need to go and consult with Vanessa about our work at UCH tomorrow, so I had better make myself scarce. The day after tomorrow, Vanessa and I will be examining the swabs we took in McTavish ward, Mel – do you want to see how we make microscope slides and examine them?"

"Oh indeed, Imogen, this is all extremely fascinating – and you never know, we might discover something relevant to Alex and my enquiries, too. Will you pick me up with the Brough then?"

Chapter 11

The telephone rang then and Melpomene, picked it up. It was Marjorie, who asked, "Are we still running an agency here? We haven't seen you or Alex for so long we were beginning to wonder!"

"Well we haven't been slacking off, I can assure you! We'll be in first thing tomorrow. Has anything of interest happened while we've been away from the office? Telephone calls? Visitors? New clients?"

"To take the last first," said Marjorie, "Winnie did talk to someone who came in this morning with an enquiry. I'll put her on and she can tell you all about it."

"I'm doubtful that this is going to amount to anything, Mel," said Winnie, "but I'm not a detective, so I didn't commit us one way or the other – she will come in tomorrow morning after nine o'clock, when I said one or both of our principals would be in. The client was a middle-aged lady, quite well-dressed, carrying a little fluffy white dog that she obviously doted on. But her enquiry was not about little Rupert, thank goodness! What was bothering Mrs Pratt-Smithers was an altercation she had just had with the dispenser at her local chemists' shop. She had taken in a prescription from her doctor, who she said was a very reliable man she had been going to for years. The woman behind the counter had accepted the script and taken it to the back where the pharmacist was working. After a few minutes he came out and asked Mrs Pratt-Smithers if she was the person for whom the script had been written, and then said that he was very puzzled because the medicine called for was a potentially dangerous barbiturate. He asked her permission to telephone her doctor and check with him – at which our client took umbrage, grabbed back the script and stormed out, saying 'How dare he question a professional medical practitioner!'. What she wants us to do is investigate this pharmacist and check whether or not he is, as she suspects, a charlatan!"

"Very interesting!" said Melpomene, "I think Alex should deal with her – she may not be able to believe that a mere slip of a girl like me could be a serious investigator! What else was there today, Winnie?"

"No other potential clients, thank goodness, Mel, and the mail was all humdrum stuff – but I took a couple of telephone calls you or Alex might be interested in. Your Mama rang at about lunchtime – nothing serious, she said, but could you ring her back and just let her know how things are going. And there was someone wanting Alex – he said he was an old acquaintance from University College, now a barrister, and simply wanted to talk over old times and catch up. His name is Monty Petherick – I wrote down his number. I think he'll keep until tomorrow, but I'll give you it now, in case Alex would like to attend to him straight away."

"Thanks, Winnie, I'll put Alex on and you can tell him. I'll call Mama before I forget again!"

While Melpomene was chatting with Lady Cynthia, Alex was racking his brains, trying to remember what it was about Petherick that had made him feel uneasy as soon as Winnie had mentioned his name. He decided to sleep on it and it might come to him.

Since there seemed to be no more business and no immediate planning to be done, the two turned to their usual relaxations, crosswords and detective novels. An hour later, Alex shut '*The Murder of Roger Ackroyd*' with a snort, saying to Mel, "Christie has led us all up the garden path until the very end, when she produces a completely unexpected villain! I think I shall start reading ancient history instead! But she has done me one favour – I have just remembered what was bothering me about Monty Petherick!"

"Oh yes, Alex, what was that, then?"

"At the end of second year law, there was an exam on jurisprudence that we were all dreading – the lecturer rambled all the time, and the references he gave us were unhelpful, to say the least! So Monty confided in me and another chap that he was going to take certain steps – without coming clean what they were to be, however much we pestered him! Anyway, when the results were posted, he had collected a score that was at least ten marks ahead of anyone else in the class, including me. Of course, we were all begging him to tell us how he did it, but he just looked smug and refused to tell!"

"Did you ever find out?" asked Mel.

"No, none of us did for sure – but the two leading conjectures were that either he had burgled the lecturer's office and copied the examination papers – that was my first guess – or that he had blackmailed him to give him a high mark! My friend Archie Staples reckoned that Monty had been seen in a pub with the lecturer's wife, and fantasized all sorts of plots based on that, but there was no way of finding out the truth of any of it. And I'm certainly not going to raise the topic when I see Monty – that's if I do agree to meet him! Come to think of it, why don't I ring Archie? I'm pretty sure I still have his number – he gave it to me when we were both playing in the European Lawyers' Amateur Golf Championship at Enfield a few weeks ago. That event was almost a University College law students' reunion!"

Alex got hold of his little black notebook and was soon dialling Archie's number. He was disappointed when Mrs Staples answered and said that her husband was talking to a solicitor about a case slated to be in the High Court soon and didn't want to be interrupted, however, she went on, "I don't think you remember me, Alex, do you? We actually went to the pictures together, with some others, a few times – I was Betty Bunton, then – Buttoned-up Betty was what you all called me! You would hardly believe it, but Archie will be taking silk in a month or two, so there will be a KC in the family! I'm quite content to carry on being a family solicitor – how about you, Alex?"

Alex explained where his career had led him, without disclosing much about their current case, and then Betty said, "You must bring your wife round for dinner some time soon and we can all share exciting anecdotes! We live in Muswell Hill, not far from Alexandra Palace, I'll get Archie to telephone you as soon as he has disposed of his solicitor. Tell me your number, Alex – I do hope you can find the time to come, I'm a bit bored with our current set!"

When Melpomene was told all this, she was quite enthusiastic, too, and said that they mustn't let the opportunity slip, "However busy we are, we should be careful to keep our social lives bubbling along, Alex – all work and no play ... as they say in the trade!"

At that point, Mrs Mountain announced dinner, "I'm giving you rabbit pie tonight. Caroline and I will help eat it, but you can't reheat a pie, so it'll all have to go tonight!

Chapter 12

As they had promised, Melpomene and Alex arrived in the office well before nine o'clock, and soon afterwards, Mrs Pratt-Smithers was let in by Winnie, who introduced her to Alex and Mel.

Alex admired her little dog, who was still clasped in her arms, and led her into the back office and made her comfortable in one of the guest chairs. "Now, can I offer you a cup of tea or coffee before we start, Mrs Pratt-Smithers?"

"That's uncommonly civil of you, Mr Crabbe, you wouldn't have Earl Grey, would you? Oh, good! No milk and just a half-teaspoon of sugar."

Once she was sipping her tea and nibbling a Garibaldi biscuit, Alex explained, "My secretary, Miss Morris, has given me a brief account of your problem, Mrs Pratt-Smithers – did you bring the offending prescription with you, by any chance?"

"I certainly did, Mr Crabbe, let me see now – sorry Rupert, just sit nicely on my lap for a moment, Mummy has to get to her handbag – yes, here we are!"

The script was hand-written on a printed form in the usual atrocious style affected by the medical profession – Alex privately thought this was a deliberate ploy to maintain a certain mystery – but he was able to make out that the medicine was specified as '*Donnatal: 25 tablets of 3/4 grain*' and there were notations about dosage and frequency.

"The signature, Madam, appears to be 'L. M. Jenkins, MD' – have I read it right?"

"Oh, yes – I have been going to him for some time now, since I lost my poor husband, four years ago – Dr Jenkins was practicing from the same address for two decades before I came to the district, I'm told."

"And, if it not impertinent to ask, would you tell me the condition for which the medicine has been prescribed? I would need this information were I to seek further professional advice from a qualified hospital pharmacist whom I often consult. You will understand that, as an investigator, I must explore all avenues, while, as a solicitor in good standing, I maintain strict confidentiality."

"I quite appreciate that, Mr Crabbe, and I have no hesitation in telling you that Dr Jenkins prescribed this for anxiety and insomnia, to replace Valerian, a herbal preparation, which I had found was no longer effective."

"I understand. Finally, Mrs Pratt-Smithers, would you tell me the name of the chemist's establishment whose pharmacist offended you? I have the doctor's name and address from the prescription, of course."

"Certainly, it was the branch of Timothy Whites' in High Street, Peckham. They employ several dispensers there, I believe, but the one who spoke to me was elderly, wearing a goatee – a foolish affectation, in my opinion!"

"Thank you for all this information, Madam. Leave it with me and I will get back to you as soon as I have worthwhile findings. Please make sure that Miss Morris has your address and telephone number. Unless you wish to say anything more, I bid you good morning!" and he shook her hand and patted Rupert's head as he showed her to the front office and Winnie.

"Nice dog!" said Melpomene, "I would prefer something a bit larger!" was Alex' reply, "Like a boxer or a beagle, or even a standard poodle! But I think we need a place with a garden before we acquire a pet – if we lived in the suburbs it would be different. So, my love, what's on the agenda today?"

"I'm not doing anything with Imogen until tomorrow, Alex, so I thought I might indulge myself in a little shopping – and I'm overdue for a visit to the hairdresser – I think I'll keep on patronising Lucy Stafford's salon – she was so helpful over changing me from a blonde to a brunette and back again! Who knows, I might have occasion to become a redhead or someone with raven locks for a future adventure – but today all I want is a trim, a shampoo and to have my curls tightened up!"

"Will you need the Riley, Mel, or can you manage that all by the tube? I wouldn't mind the car today, I have plans to visit some pharmaceutical suppliers – particularly Katzenberg Ethicals and Hardcastle Brothers, in the guise of a continental drug manufacturer looking for distributors."

"Oh dear, I have two worries about that, Alex – first, how will you avoid running into people you've already met in another guise – and second, what makes you think you know enough about drugs to play a convincing role as a manufacturer!"

"The first of your worries is not going to occur, I think, Mel. I have, it's true, been in the same room as Dodson, the Katzenberg rep who was talking to our rural Dean, Jackson, over lunch at the hospital, but I have no reason to believe he took any notice of me – we were at opposite sides of the common-room after all. As for the second of your concerns, I am an English agent working on behalf of a continental manufacturing firm and I have simply been asked by my management to make some enquiries of likely suppliers – I shall disclaim any detailed technical knowledge. I think I'm a good enough bluffer to string this story along quite a way! And Marjorie is typing me up a copy of a pharmaceutical catalogue that I asked Elspeth to lend me, so I can show my prospects sample pages without disclosing that they come from another firm."

"So will you just telephone them cold, as it were? Have you picked out a fictitious firm to represent? Do you want to try your act out on me, Alex, so I can pick holes in it if there be any!"

"Think about this, then, Mel. I am representing Dwyer, Sanderson and Philby, whose head office is in Newcastle. They have contracts with French and German suppliers that cover various areas in the North, but have not yet been able to penetrate very far into the market around London and the home counties, so they have given me the job of creating interest in wholesalers down here. Katzenberg Ethicals is the first stop on my itinerary – I am not at liberty to disclose who else I shall be visiting. What I would like to do is to find out whether the firms I approach have a sufficiently extensive market with hospitals and retail chemists' chains that it will be worthwhile spending money and time to develop relationships, which will probably depend on the appointment of resident liaison managers in these wholesale firms, like Katzenberg's."

"That sounds as though you know what you are doing, Alex! If I didn't know you I might very well be convinced, especially were I a greedy sales manager looking to increase my company's profits! – I don't know why you didn't decide to become a barrister, Alex my love – you lie so convincingly that you would convince any judge and jury!"

Chapter 13

"Before we leave the office on our various errands," said Alex, "I ought to ring Monty Petherick and see what he's on about – I'll try to get more information from Archie before I actually take it any further – I still feel pretty cagey about him! Could you try Petherick's number for me, please, Winnie?"

Monty Petherick was very effusive when Alex spoke to him, "It seems ages since we saw each other last – it was probably at graduation, wasn't it? When I saw your name and the name of your agency in the phone book, I thought I would look you up – partly to chat about old times, but also because I have a puzzling situation developing with a character I shall be defending soon on a charge of drug dealing. If you are willing and up to it, I wondered whether you would do a little bit of digging for me. The client has plenty of money, so there would be no trouble covering your fees and expenses. Can I meet you somewhere mutually convenient? I see your office is rather distant from the Law Courts, and I need to stay accessible so my clerk can fetch me at short notice. How about if we meet in a coffee-house near by or somewhere like that?"

"There's a pleasant little place in the Strand, called 'Cakes and Ale' not far from the Courts – how about that?"

"Super! – I'm in court tomorrow on a different case, but that judge always adjourns in plenty of time for lunch, so how about meeting at noon? You'll probably still recognise me, even with my wig and gown!"

As Alex finished his call, Melpomene, too, was putting her telephone down, "That was Betty Staples, Alex, saying that she and her husband were quite eager to see us, and could we make it to their place this very evening! So I said yes – I hope I did right! I heard you making arrangements to see this Petherick person, so now you can get briefed about him if necessary before you meet him! Betty told me their address in Muswell Hill, and I promised to be there at about seven o'clock. We should take a bottle of wine, shouldn't we? Are they worth French champagne, do you think? I shall go straight home after the hairdresser, so I'll see you there. Try not to be too late!"

In the event, Alex arrived back at the flat at about five-thirty, with a beaming smile on his face, "Come and talk to me in the bathroom while I make myself presentable, Mel – I think I did rather well with Messrs Katzenberg! I telephoned them first and fed the person who the operator put me onto first, a Claude Houghton, the tale I related to you earlier. He listened and asked a couple of questions and then said I should talk to his departmental manager. He asked me to hold on for a moment while he spoke to him and than said that Mr Stephenson had agreed to talk to me if I could be at his office in half an hour. So I said I would, of course, and then Houghton checked that I knew where to come."

"So did you feel nervous, Alex – I would have done in the circumstances, though I find that I can usually rise to the occasion when it counts!"

"Not really, Mel, there were too many thoughts going round in my head. Anyway, when I got to the building and stated my business, I was shown, with no questions asked, into Stephenson's office. It was quite impressive – he must be rather a senior manager, which pleased me, of course – with a desk the size of a tennis court, and those deep leather armchairs they have in exclusive clubs. I went into my tale again, and he put his fingers together under his chin and nodded away, looking wise. Then he told me something that surprised me a lot – but also encouraged me greatly!"

"Come on, Alex, tell me all! You can fuss with your hair later!"

"Well the first thing he said was that he wanted to make it clear that I would have to be prepared to encounter a lot of cut-and-thrust in this field and that some companies were adopting tactics that verged on the distasteful, even if they managed to remain just within the law. I just nodded sagely, but I was thinking that maybe this would be a chance to identify some dubious practices and practitioners."

"Then what?"

"Next he pushed a piece of paper across his desk to me and said that if I wanted to do work for his company, I must sign a non-disclosure agreement. This bothered me for a moment – I have always been accustomed to sign documents as Alexander Crabbe, but then I thought that, since this was all a fiction as far as I was concerned, I would simply sign as Alan Robertson. I must say, my inner solicitor felt a bit queasy over this, but I decided to ignore him! So I signed and gave him back the paper. He looked at it briefly and put a paperweight on it. Then he asked me whether I would like a coffee or tea – I thought that this meant that I was really on board! Stephenson tinkled a little bell and a woman brought a tray. As she left, he said 'Minerva – please bring those documents I asked for and make sure Mr Robertson takes them away with him!' "

Melpomene had been following all this in great fascination, and said, "So, my darling, you have now crossed over to the dark side – you must step very carefully from now on!"

"I know, I know! Then Stephenson said that Katzenberg's were under pressure from their parent company in Luxembourg to expand their business, with hospitals generally, but especially with High Street chemist's shops – he said Boots was a lost cause, because they were big enough to source their supplies directly from the manufacturers, both in England and on the continent – and he thought I might be well-positioned to help in this. Then he stood up, came round his desk and shook hands. As I left, his secretary gave me a pile of papers, which I put straight into my case. I haven't looked at them yet, but will do so after we get back from the Staples!"

"Yes, Alex, we had better set off now. You drive, because you know where we're going. I bought a bottle of Grand Cru on the way home from the hairdressers, and it's been cooling in the frig, I hope they appreciate good champagne!"

Alex indeed had looked up the address and worked out how to get there, so they drew up outside the house only five minutes late. It was not a grand mansion, but a villa, which nevertheless exuded an atmosphere of comfortable affluence, with well-tended gardens and shrubberies around it. The doorbell was answered by a maid in standard garb, who took them to a sitting room where Betty and Archie Staples stood up and greeted them, in Betty's case by embracing Alex and kissing him warmly. Archie shook Melpomene's hand and then Alex' and waved them to a settee.

"What would you like to drink," asked Archie, "we should save your champagne for the table I think! Thank you so much for bringing it, but of course there was no need!"

They were soon all four sipping aperitifs, the men chatting about old times while Betty quizzed Mel about being a detective, which she guessed was more exciting than her own humdrum life as a family solicitor. After a while the maid announced that dinner was served, and they all moved out.

Chapter 14

Over dinner, the conversation ranged widely, starting with reminiscences by Alex and Archie about old acquaintances at University College, and queries by Melpomene and Betty about friends they might have in common. When Mel mentioned she had been at the London School of Economics, it turned out that Betty's accountant had studied there too – but Mel and he had never crossed paths.

But by the time they had all disposed of the saddle of mutton that made up the main course and were relaxing a little over the sweets and port, the topics became more focused, and Alex asked Archie if he had had much contact with Monty Petherick since graduation, "He has just popped out of the woodwork as a prospective client, and I would like to find out a little more about him first – I've been carrying severe doubts about his honesty since that business over the Jurisprudence exam, if you remember that!"

"Oh yes, Alex, it made a long-term impression on me, too. Only a couple of years ago I was prosecuting an estate agent accused of misappropriating clients' funds, and Monty was defending him! The case he made was that several hundred pounds had been lodged by the buyer with the agent so that he could advance a deposit to secure the purchase being negotiated, and that it had been duly so advanced, as he had been instructed. Unfortunately for the agent, he had inadvertently paid it into the account at his local bank of a completely different person, who subsequently claimed it was legitimately his! After a lot more business, Monty was able to convince the court that it was all a genuine mistake, and the case was dismissed after the funds had been returned to the buyer! At the time I was very suspicious, but I was unable to make any headway and we simply had to shrug it off. I vowed that if I ever found myself up against Petherick again I would recuse myself! I would advise you, Alex, to check everything very carefully before you take on Monty as a client!"

"Thanks, Archie, I am very grateful for that! But I have an ulterior motive for considering him. He says he is defending someone on a charge of drug dealing, and I would like to use this as an opportunity to find out more about that business, since it might impinge on another case we are running at the moment. I can't say any more, and it might come to nothing, anyway!"

After enjoying the dinner they all withdrew – the men to Archie's recently-acquired pride and joy, his billiard table – where Alex discovered that he still retained some of the skills of his student days, while Betty showed Melpomene her attempts at watercolour landscapes, which she was inclined to modestly disparage. Mel assured her that she had seen much inferior works sold for good prices at auction, "I can put you in touch with a gallery director we know who will tell you the same, Betty!"

"When I have a little more free time, perhaps, Melpomene, I seem to be coping with a deluge of clients at the moment – not that I can complain! It will be a while before Archie is known well enough to be instructed by solicitors on a frequent basis – maybe he will do better when he has taken silk!"

The time flew by until Alex looked at his watch and said, "We shall have to love you and leave you now, since we have business to attend to in the morning. I can't remember when I enjoyed an evening as much – you must come to us next time!"

When they got back to the flat, Alex said, "I should really look at the papers I got from Stephenson at Katzenberg's, but I'm a bit tired, so I'll leave if for the morning. What are you up to tomorrow – off to the lab again, isn't it?"

"That's right, and I must also remember to see whether I can talk to Gordon Salmon some time about the duty rotas – I could just ask Matron Stevenson or Sister Wood, but I'd rather keep the extent of my activities as private as possible for a while. We'll have to be careful to keep all these Stevensons and Stephensons separated in our minds! I'll try and find out about the catering services, too."

"And I'll have to work out how I shall tackle Monty Petherick," said Alex, "I'll try and pump him without disclosing my own agenda of course – this promises to be an interesting conversation! I'm not seeing him until noon, so that gives me plenty of pondering time. I might try looking up his case in the Fortnightly Law Digest tomorrow morning – it might have been mentioned in court already, for remand or something. But I mustn't think about it now, or I shall dream about it all night – unless you can think of a way of distracting me, Mel!"

Over breakfast, Melpomene asked Alex whether she should ask Matron or Sister Wood about the duty rotas, or wait until she could speak to Gordon Salmon. "I don't think this is a particularly sensitive matter, Mel," he replied, "you won't need to make lengthy explanations to either of them, unless they start getting picky. As Imogen's research assistant you might very well need to study the rotas in connection with your sampling. Just ask whoever is most convenient! There will probably be other ward sisters to see, too."

"I'm going to the lab first, Alex, as soon as Imogen picks me up, so I'll see if she is happy with that – I can't really do swab collection without her, in any case. What will you do before you go and meet Monty Petherick? Could you find out about the catering services for me? You've broken the ice with Dean Jackson, so you could ask him – he wasn't around when you tried him yesterday, was he? You might have better luck this morning. Have you got his number in your little book, or will you need to go to the office?"

The telephone rang, Alex answered, and it was Imogen, saying, "Please apologize to Mel and say I can't pick her up today, because the Brough is out of commission – the chain broke and the local garages don't keep that size, so I'm having one sent from the Brough factory in Nottingham. It is being sent by train, so I'll have to go to Kings Cross station to pick it up from the train arriving at 11.30. Perhaps I'd better talk to her, Alex."

Melpomene took the telephone, "No worries, Imogen, I'll pick you up from your place and run you to the station in the Riley. Alex will be OK going to his appointment by Tube – won't you Alex? He's nodding, Imogen, so tell me where you live and I'll pick you up. OK, I'll write that down. See you soon! I'll come to the door, no need to hang about in the street!"

"Oh good! Vanessa was only saying this morning that she wanted to have a chat – she wasn't able to come to the lab when you were there last time and she was sorry she missed you. It won't take you very long to get here, and the train doesn't get in until 11.30, so we can have a cup of tea or coffee and chat over it."

"I'll bring some jam tarts, I am suffering a deficiency of them at the moment! Unless you would prefer something else? Does Vanessa indulge in anything sinful like that? Right, I'll be there in a flash!"

42

Chapter 15

Vanessa and Imogen lived in a rather modest mews off one of the streets near Knightsbridge, and when Mel drew up she saw Imogen fussing over her Brough Superior in what had been the stable. She straightened up and welcomed Mel, saying, "I won't shake hands yet, they're all greasy – I've been getting things ready for the new chain. Go up the outside stairs there – I think Vanessa has the kettle on – and I'll be up in a moment. Your Riley will be all right where it is."

Over tea and the promised jam tarts the three had an enjoyable chat, and it seemed no time before Imogen glanced at her watch and said, "We should be off soon, but it will not take very long to get to Kings Cross. I don't know about parking, though."

Melpomene said, "If it's difficult, I'll just wait in the street while you pop in – we shall see. Can I use your telephone first, please? I want to see what Alex has found out – he was making a few enquiries before he goes to the Law Courts at noon."

"Be our guest, Mel, the telephone is in the hall. Just through there."

Alex answered immediately, but before Mel could say much, he exclaimed, "We have lost a client already – the police have just rung – Mrs Pratt-Smithers had one of our cards on her bedside table and when her body was discovered they didn't have a lot to go on and telephoned me at the office! But I will start at the beginning, like a good detective should! What happened was this – early this morning, Mrs Pratt-Smithers' next-door neighbour, Mrs Dugdale, heard Rupert, the little dog, whining and carrying on for a long time, so after a while she went and knocked. Mrs P-S has no live-in servants, just a daily, who arrived just as the neighbour was knocking, heard her explanation, and let them both in. They could still hear Rupert crying, from the bedroom by the sound of it, so the daily went upstairs and knocked, while Mrs Dugdale waited in the hall. There was no answer, so the daily went into the bedroom. Immediately, she gave a great screech and rushed out, so Mrs Dugdale went up to see. The long and the short of it was that Mrs Pratt-Smithers was found lying dead in her bed, with Rupert frantically licking her face. The police were called and were happy to tell me all this, since our reputation is known

43

throughout the whole force, apparently! I've arranged to go to see them this afternoon, once I've finished with Monty Petherick. How about that, Mel!"

"Amazing, Alex, I can hardly wait for the next exciting episode – but I've got to take Imogen and Vanessa to Kings Cross now and then go on to UC, so I'll see you at home this evening – after you've seen the police! Will you let Jimmy Manley know?"

She was tempted to tell the others, but thought she had better leave it until later, "Are we ready, yet, ladies? Let's head for the station!"

At Kings Cross station, as Imogen had predicted, parking was difficult, so she nipped in while Mel and Vanessa waited in the car at the kerb. Less then ten minutes later Imogen was back, carrying a parcel, and they set off for University College.

Out of the Petri dishes that had been seeded on the previous visit, only half a dozen were showing any signs of colonies of bacteria. "This is about par for the course," said Vanessa, "so Imogen will show you what we do next."

Imogen took a wire loop with wooden handle and heated the loop at the business end to a red heat. Then she waved it about to cool it off, before scooping up some of the colony and smearing it onto a glass microscope slide, adding a drop of stain and covering it with a thin glass slip.

"Now let's see what we can see under the binocular microscope," she said and showed Mel how to put the slide on the stage and clip it down. "It may take you a while to get a good focus, Mel," she said, "close one eye to start with and then twiddle till the image comes clear. Then you can bring the other image up and see what you can discover."

All Mel could see were a few vague blobs, so Vanessa explained that it might take a few months of practice to train someone on what to look for. Mel was quiet happy to leave it at that, saying that she had no illusions about her skills and would gladly leave it to the experts!

Vanessa lent her some folders of micrographs to look at while she and Imogen examined the remaining samples. After an hour or two, Vanessa said that they had finished for the day. "So, what we have found is that, out of the patients in McTavish Ward on that day, one might be infected with a dangerous strain of Staphylococcus, but will need further tests, and three have an invasion of a common yeast in their mouths, which is of no real concern – we all get it from time to time! But this all goes into our research data records, so we are by no means disappointed. Thank you, Melpomene, I hope you will have the time to help Imogen again soon. Now let's go to the student refectory and see about a modest lunch – my treat!"

Over lunch, Melpomene decided she might as well take the opportunity to ask Vanessa about Mrs Pratt-Smithers' medication, "Vanessa, are you familiar with a drug called Donnatal? One of our clients was prescribed it for insomnia and anxiety."

"Yes, Mel, that is a barbiturate – but I would think it rather like taking a sledgehammer to crack an egg to use it for insomnia. You would have to make sure the dosage was very low."

"Like three-quarters of a grain, Vanessa?"

"Yes, that's quite moderate, providing the patient only took one at a time. Has your client been experiencing any difficulty with it?"

"She's not experiencing anything right now – she's dead!"

"From your questioning, am I to assume that you suspect that the Donnatal caused her demise, Melpomene – what has the post-mortem found?"

"The death was only discovered this morning, Vanessa, so I doubt that any investigation has been possible yet – Alex told me about it when I telephoned him from your place this morning!"

"As a doctor and a scientist, I like to consider everything as a possibility." said Vanessa, "This could be an accidental overdose, or it could be suicide – did your client appear depressed at all – you said she was taking the medicine for anxiety? And the other possibility, of course, is murder!"

"We can't discount this, of course – we have had experience of murder several times in our practice, not long ago, either! But we shouldn't jump to any conclusions until we have found out much more! Now, are you ready to be taken home? I love your mews house by the way – I'll have to talk about it with Alex – we are both feeling ready for a change of abode."

"You should be quick, then, mews places are getting very fashionable lately, so the prices are sky-rocketing!"

Chapter 16

After dropping Vanessa and Imogen home, Mel drove to the office on the assumption that Alex would go there after his talk with Monty Petherick, but Marjorie said that neither she nor Winnie had seen him yet.

"But Jimmy Manley called half an hour ago, Mel – and said could you telephone him as soon as you got in. He had spoken to Alex earlier, who said he was on his way to Finchley Hospital, where Mrs Pratt-Smithers' body had been taken for autopsy. But he'll tell you all the details when you ring."

Jimmy answered his phone straight away, saying, "Nice to hear that you and Alex are not content with dull routine, Mel! I've been briefed by the uniformed sergeant who was called to the dead woman's house by the neighbour – Mrs Dugdale I think is her name – the charwoman was having conniptions so wasn't in any state to communicate clearly. As well as helping the police and settling the daily down with a cup of tea, Mrs Dugdale has taken charge of the little dog, which was good of her."

"Oh, I did worry a bit about the dog, Jimmy – I thought it was a nice little thing, even though I prefer them a bit bigger!"

"Sergeant Hancock sounded as though he had everything well organised – he's left a PC at the house to make sure nothing gets touched until the scientific squad have done their thing, except that he has taken charge of a bottle of pills that was on the bedside table. All that's been done so far is to put the unfortunate lady on a stretcher and take her to the morgue at Finchley Hospital where the PM will be performed by a staff pathologist. Your friend Gordon Salmon will assist him, I believe. And Alex has gone to the hospital to see what results they come up with."

"What about the pills, Jimmy, is anyone checking them to check whether or not they are the ones that were prescribed?"

"You are certainly on the ball, Mel! They have been sent, by police motorcycle courier, to the Metropolitan Police Lab at Lambeth, who will check the content and strength of the pills. They will send me their report, probably later today or early tomorrow – I'm a favoured customer there!"

"Thanks for all that, Jimmy – I shall now go to the hospital and see what's what. I'd better try not to be spotted by Matron – I don't want to risk my cover as Henrietta Musgrave, research assistant, being blown!"

Mel parked near the emergency entrance of Finchley Hospital and asked the attendant at the reception counter where she would find the mortuary and the post-mortem suite.

"Are you the relative of a deceased, Madam? Access to those areas is restricted, as you might suppose."

"No, but the police are involved, and I am a Special Constable – here is my warrant card. I'm also known to Dr Gordon Salmon, who I believe is assisting in the PM – who is doing that, by the way?"

"I saw Dr Aitcheson arrive an hour ago – he is the consultant pathologist who often performs autopsies. I will get a porter to take you there, it is not easy to find, being in the basement."

Melpomene was taken down service stairs and along a corridor to the mortuary, where there was a man in a grey dustcoat sitting reading the racing pages of the evening paper.

She told him her business, to which he said, "Let me check first, Madam, to see whether the doctors are willing to have you present."

He disappeared through a door and then came back, helped her on with a white overall, and beckoned her in. Surrounding a large zinc-covered work table she saw Alex, Gordon Salmon, and a tall grey-haired man who was at the point of making an incision in the abdomen of a corpse, almost completely covered in green drapes.

"How strong is your stomach, Madam? Your husband has told me you are robust in most ways, but I don't wish to see you upset by what I am about to do. Please think hard before you stay and watch – it will not be long before I can tell all of you what little I have discovered – all that is left is for me to sample the stomach contents for analysis, which is what we shall rely on for the definitive answer."

"Thank you, Doctor," said Mel, "maybe I will withdraw after all. I will wait outside!"

She borrowed the paper from the attendant and turned to the crossword. It was a very simple one, not cryptic, and she

47

knocked it off in a few minutes, so she was pleased to see the others emerge from the autopsy room.

The pathologist, Dr Aitcheson, said, "These are only preliminary findings – we need the results of the analysis of stomach contents, and of the pills this lady ingested – but my present opinion is that her demise was the result of an inadvertent or deliberate overdose, hence accident or suicide. I could find no bruises or other evidence of force being used on her, except for some minor animal scratches on her lower arms, probably caused by the lady's pet dog. Please don't quote me on this until we have the other evidence!"

Alex said, "Thank you very much, Doctor. When can we expect to find out about the stomach contents? I was told that the laboratory assay of the pills might be available from the Lambeth police lab early tomorrow, all going well. I expect that Detective-Inspector Manley, of Mile End Road station, who has taken charge of the official aspects of this investigation, will confer with you once the results are known, so that you will be in a position to make an official report for the Coroner."

Mel, Alex and Gordon Salmon thanked and shook hands with the pathologist and walked together back to the ambulance entrance.

Alex said, "I'll go into my meeting with Monty Petherick fully at home, Mel, but I will tell you both that it added another piece to the jigsaw puzzle I'm slowly assembling on the activities of dubious pharmaceutical suppliers! I casually mentioned the name of Katzenbergs as he was telling me about his current case with the drug dealer, and I thought he started a little – I didn't persist and he went on with his story. Maybe this was meaningful, maybe not!"

As they got into the Riley, Gordon unlocked his bicycle from a railing near by and said, "I hope you enjoyed the entertainment we just put on – but please do not bring me any more post-mortems for a while – I much prefer dealing with the living, however knocked about they are when I see them!"

Mel and Alex were soon home, and fell on cups of tea as though they were just back from the desert, then chatted as they anticipated enjoying one of Mrs Mountain's constructions, which she described as "Corned beef 'ash, with pertaters O'Grady". It was, of course, delicious!

Chapter 17

After dinner, Alex described how his meeting with Monty Petherick had gone.

"I waited in the Cakes and Ale restaurant for twenty minutes, starting to wonder whether I had been stood up, but then Monty arrived in his wig and gown, looking a bit flustered. He spotted me immediately, sat down at my table and beckoned the waiter, saying. 'What do you fancy, Spider? Oh, perhaps you think it infra dig to use your old college nickname? Alex it is then – what will you have? They do a good mixed grill here.' I said that would be fine, and we should have a bottle of something red with it, in celebration of old times. We reminisced for a few moments, and then he came to the point, telling me about a fellow he was about to defend on a charge of drug dealing."

"So the case hasn't started yet?" asked Mel, "No, he has had some conferences with the defendant and his solicitor in a cell at the remand centre – the police are being very serious about it and bail has been refused. The man was stopped at Dover leaving a cross-channel ferry from Calais with an ordinary steamer trunk containing a large quantity of various barbiturates and opiates, even including tins of raw opium. He protested that he was a legitimate agent of a wholesale pharmaceutical supply company, but could not explain why he had no import licence with him, so Customs called the police and he was taken in charge."

"Did he name the wholesalers, Alex?"

"Monty didn't say – I think he realised he had already disclosed more than he should. But later on in the conversation, I casually mentioned Katzenberg's while watching him closely, and I think I saw a spark of recognition there! I passed over it and asked him what he had in mind for us to do, and then he opened up freely. As the barrister assigned to the defence, there are restrictions on who he can talk to outside court – members of the jury, of course, witnesses already called by the prosecution and those on the bench, including the judge himself. What he wants me – or you – to do, is to talk to anyone we think might provide information useful to the defence."

"Did he suggest anyone in particular at this point, Alex? Or does he just want us to find witnesses or experts who might be valuable?"

"I asked him directly, Mel, and he gave me a list that he had already prepared. I just put it in my notebook, telling him that I would peruse it thoroughly later. He nodded at this, saying that he agreed with a careful approach, but adding that if we needed any funds to pursue our enquiries, we should not feel the need to check with him beforehand, as his client's firm was prepared to support the case to any reasonable extent."

"Oh, good, Alex! We can go to Switzerland to find some of these people – it says in the paper that there have been good snowfalls in the popular resorts there!"

"Good try, my darling! But let's be a little more realistic to start with. Where's that list – ah, here we are. He has listed quite a few names, see, some of them with their firm and their position, others with a rough description of where they might be found, for instance, '*Clarrie Pusey: Client alleges that he is a known drug-dealer whose headquarters is the private bar of the Marquis of Sketchley pub in Rotherhithe.*' Could make an interesting visit – but it sounds as though one would need to have a pistol with one – these dockland pubs are the haunts of all sorts of disreputable characters, I'm told!"

"Always pubs, Alex! I should write something up for a Social Anthropology journal!"

Alex went on, "But, this is interesting, too, further down the list is an entry that jumps out at me, '*Claude Houghton, assistant to the General Manager, Katzenberg's. Please tread warily with this man!*' As you may recall, I spoke to him before I had my interview with Stephenson!"

"And, I also recall that Stephenson gave you a pile of papers, Alex. Have you had a chance to go through them yet?"

"No, but I will do so straight away! This also means that I have an established cover story with him, so if we want to investigate him on Monty's behalf, you will have to do it, Mel!"

"Let's go through the rest of Monty's list, first, Alex, before we embark on the Stephenson papers – otherwise it will become even more confusing than it is already. But what we chiefly need is a transfusion of tea before we proceed further – we could be in for a late night!"

After they had had their cups of tea and some rather elderly jam tarts, Melpomene spread out a sheet of cartridge paper on the table, found her coloured pencils and started constructing one of her favourite charts.

"I'm writing the names of the good in blue, Alex, and the ungodly in red. I'm doing those we're unsure of in ordinary pencil, so they can be rubbed out and changed one way or the other as we find out more about them."

"Let me see, Mel. I assume you're not putting the police on yet? Here we are – Gordon Salmon is in blue, obviously, so is Elspeth McCracken, and Sister Wood – but Matron Stevenson is in pencil! That's a bit cautious of you, isn't it? Then we have some red ones – Henry Jackson the Rural Dean, and Stephenson, of course, as well as Claude Houghton, as his associate and Dodson, the Adolphe Menjou look-alike, all from Katzenberg's. By the time you've got all of Monty Petherick's list on the chart, it will grow considerably!"

"Oh, Alex, I think I'll need another colour for victims! Green I think. There's poor Mrs Pratt-Smithers for a start – Oh, I should add Dr Aitcheson the pathologist – pencil I think, just to be on the safe side! And Monty's defendant I'll put in red, because he's a putative villain – what's his name, the man with the trunk. I'll just put trunk-man for the present."

"Once we're in the office, we can look up his name in the Fortnightly Law Digest – even if Monty's case hasn't started properly, the man was remanded in custody and refused bail, so that should be listed. And don't forget the mysterious Clarrie Pusey and anyone else of a doubtful nature on Monty's list – all in red, I reckon. Have you got Monty himself? He sounds like a red one, if you ask me!"

This sort of discussion went on until Melpomene yawned, stood up and said, "I'm going to have a cup of chocolate and a bath right now and hit the pillow! Don't stay up too late Alex, otherwise you will be worthless in the morning! Chocolate for you, too?"

"Yes, Mel, of course you're right. I'll leave this all on the table. Caroline knows not to tidy away any papers after that incident during her first week. I must say, though, she cheerfully scrabbled through the dustbins and got everything back, plus a few tea-leaves. We're very lucky to have her and Mrs M!"

51

Chapter 18

When Melpomene and Alex arrived at the office, a little later than usual, they were met by an excited Winnie, waving an envelope. "This was delivered by a man just now – he said it was a summons for Mr and Mrs Crabbe. He wanted to wait, but I assured him it would be given to you as soon as you arrived, and he shrugged and left, saying, 'Please sign for it, then.' Have you got into trouble with the police?"

Alex took the envelope from her, opened it and read it.

"It's a summons for us both to attend the inquest on Mrs Pratt-Smithers, at 11 am at the North London Coroner's Court in High Barnet. We'd better get a wiggle on, although it's not all that far. I think all we know is in our heads, so we don't need to take any papers. I wonder who else they've called?"

"Before we go," said Mel, "have there been any other calls?"

"Not so far, Mel. How long will you be away?"

"All depends, Winnie! We'll try and make it back before nightfall!"

They arrived at the building in good time and were shown into the court, after giving their names and signing a book, and saw that there were already several people they knew sitting waiting – Detective-Inspector Jimmy Manley, a uniformed sergeant and another policeman, and Dr Aitcheson, the pathologist from Finchley Hospital, and Gordon Salmon. As well there were some strangers, two middle-aged women – one of them crying and dabbing her eyes – and a bespectacled man holding a folder full of papers.

Then a clerk appeared from a door behind the bench and said "All rise – Dr Wilfred Collins, presiding." Then the coroner entered and bowed, took his seat, and everyone sat down. He nodded to the clerk, who said, "Is Mrs Jemima Hudson present? Good, please take the stand, hold the Bible in your hand and read the oath from the card."

The tearful woman complied, and seeing she was anxious, the Coroner said, "Please don't be nervous, Mrs Hudson, I would like you to tell me in your own words, how you discovered the unfortunate deceased person, Mrs Clarissa Pratt-Smithers. Take your time. State your name and circumstances first, please."

"Yes, your worship, me name is Mrs Jemima Ruth Hudson, widow, and I oblige – used to oblige – Mrs Pratt-Smithers every day with her housework and such, including cooking luncheon and dinner for her. On that day I arrived at me usual time and saw Mrs Dugdale standing on the front step ringing the bell. She aksed me if I could hear the little dog carrying on – Rupert is 'is name, he's – was – Mrs Smithers' pride and joy – she hasn't got no children I believe – and I said 'what was his problem?', and unlocked the door for us. We could hear that he was crying in the bedroom, so I went up and knocked. When I went in I saw her in bed, with the dog a-licking of her face, and knew she was dead, poor soul. I don't remember what I did then, I was overcome, like, so Mrs Dugdale took over and called the police and everything."

She burst into tears, and the Coroner said, "Thank you very much, Mrs Hudson, you've done well. Please take your seat now, and if I want anything else from you it can wait a little. I will hear from Mrs Dugdale, now, Mr Hatton."

She confirmed Mrs Hudson's account and told how she had sent for the police. The proceedings continued, with the police sergeant and his companion giving their accounts of what they discovered and how the ambulance was called to take the body to the mortuary.

At last, Dr Aitcheson took the stand and made his report on the autopsy, saying that there were no signs of violence, but that the pupils were highly dilated and so he suspected an overdose of the barbiturate medicine, but apart from that, all he could do was to take samples of blood and stomach contents, since the bladder was empty. "I understood that the police had taken charge of a bottle of tablets found on the bedside table and would send them to the Metropolitan Police Laboratory for testing, so all I could do then was wait for results of the analysis of the blood and stomach contents and of the tests on the pills."

"And, Doctor, have you received these yet?"

"Only the stomach analysis, your honour, I believe that Detective-Inspector Manley will report on the pills. The stomach contents, with the expected food residues, revealed no evidence of medications. I expected this, since barbiturates are absorbed into the blood stream almost immediately after

53

ingestion. Blood tests take a few days, so they are not yet available."

"Thank you, Doctor, we shall have to be patient. I would now be interested to hear from Detective-Inspector Manley."

Jimmy reported that the Police Laboratory had found that the tablets were indeed, as prescribed, Donnatal, but that they had told him that this medicine was not normally prescribed for anxiety or insomnia, but for digestive problems, since, as well as the barbiturate, it contained components derived from belladonna. And, furthermore, although the prescription had been for ¾ grain tablets, the ones they examined had over 3 grains of phenobarbitone per tablet, a potentially dangerous dose. The laboratory supervisor said that the doctor who prescribed it, a Dr L. M. Jenkins, and the pharmacists who made it up, Latham and Sons, of 24 High Street Peckham, should be interrogated about this without delay.

"She should have stuck with Timothy Whites!" Melpomene whispered to Alex.

Jimmy went on, "I visited Dr Jenkins during his evening surgery last night and put this to him. He was at first irate at the accusation, but when I soothed him, he took his prescription pad and leaved through the carbons until he found the copy of the script. He then turned pale and said 'How could I have done this – I was sure I wrote Veronal, not Donnatal! – I must telephone the patient and tell her not to have the script made up!' I, of course, told him he was too late!"

The coroner than said to his clerk, "Was not Dr Jenkins served notice to attend today?"

"Yes, sir, but I haven't seen him, and the notice was successfully hand-delivered – I will follow this up urgently, as soon as you adjourn the hearing."

"In that case, ladies and gentlemen," said the coroner, "I now adjourn this inquest, to be reconvened at a date and time which I shall send out. Mesdames Dugdale and Hudson, we shall not require you again – thank you both very much! Everyone else will be called when we reconvene."

The bespectacled man with the folder, who Mel and Alex had noticed when they arrived, said, "I am representing Latham and Sons, Sir, so I shall expect to be called. Meanwhile, with your permission, I shall speak to Detective Inspector Manley."

Chapter 19

Alex nudged Melpomene and whispered, "Why don't we speak to this man? We could get some good inside information, as long as we can convince him we don't want to sue the chemists."

As they left the court, they saw the man in conversation with Jimmy Manley, who raised his eyebrows when he saw Mel and Alex, and said, "Excuse me for a moment, Mr Hedges, I think my friends would like to hear what you have just started telling me – please let me introduce Mr and Mrs Crabbe, who are private investigators who have frequently worked with the police. Perhaps we could go and sit down in that waiting room over there."

Hedges shook their hands, saying, "Talbot Hedges – I am a solicitor with a practice in Peckham. I'll start my story again when we are seated."

They found two facing benches, and Hedges said, "As I told the Coroner, I am representing Latham and Sons, whose principal pharmacist, Edwin Stringer, dispensed the tablets in question. He pointed out that he had been surprised when he saw the prescription, as Donnatal is not frequently used nowadays, except for hospital in-patients, so he had telephoned Dr Jenkins to check, but was unable to reach him – his wife said he was out on his rounds – so he went ahead with dispensing the medication, since he could see that Mrs Pratt-Smithers was becoming exasperated at the delay."

Melpomene spoke up, "We can certainly understand that, Mr Hedges – Mrs Pratt-Smithers came to our agency, complaining that the dispenser at Timothy Whites' was being obstructive about the script. She had taken umbrage at that, and had apparently sought a more compliant pharmacist, poor soul!"

Hedges went on, "As it turns out, Mr Stringer might have done better to refuse her too – but how was he to know? He was, of course, distressed to hear from Dr Jenkins this morning about the unfortunate demise of the lady, and told his employer, Mr Douglas Latham, who immediately consulted me, fearing that one or both of them might be held accountable. I said that I would see them at the inquest – he told me the place and time – but, as we have discovered, neither he, Mr Stringer, nor the doctor have turned up. I will go round to the shop, of course, as soon as I can, but since I saw Detective-Inspector Manley was here, I thought it prudent to mention it to him."

"You did right!" said Jimmy, "There are a lot of questions that need answering, the chief of these being, to my mind, how the tablets of greater strength were supplied, when ¾ grain tablets were called for – those might have been unusual, but they wouldn't have killed her. According to our lab report, there were still 24 tablets remaining in the bottle, out of 25 prescribed, so she must only have taken one. I think Mr Stringer will have a lot of explaining to do – we know he was already dubious about the script, so it's hardly likely he would have knowingly dispensed a tablet of four times the strength!"

Alex asked, "Who would be the best person to start these enquiries? It would seem like overdoing it, for us all to arrive at the chemists' shop together! All the same, I would dearly love to find out the source of these pills, since I've already had my suspicions aroused about at least one of the local suppliers!"

"I think you've put your finger on it, Alex," said Melpomene, "there is more than one point of departure here – you are interested in tracking down dishonest suppliers – Jimmy wants to know whether anything illegal has been going on – and Mr Hedges has to think about possible cases for the defence of Messrs Stringer and Latham. We all, one way or another, want to find out what happened, and how and why!"

"There speaks the social anthropologist!" exclaimed Alex, "Mel would really like to know more than anything else how all of these lines intertwine!"

"Right you are!" said Mel, "So what I suggest is that Detective-Inspector Manley should go first, since he has his duty as a policeman to perform. Then Mr Hedges will be able to find out what charges, if any, he will have to start preparing for and see his clients, if he has any, accordingly. And Alex and I can skulk around the edges, picking up the scraps, if there are any!"

Jimmy pondered a little and then said, "Agreed! I'll go ahead on that basis, but I'll take Mr Hedges with me. When we've spoken to Mr Latham and Mr Stringer, we'll be in a much better position to judge whether there is anything sinister going on. At the moment, all we can say for certain is that some bad mistakes have been made. I'll telephone you two at your agency when I have anything to report, Mel and Alex! Did you come to the court by car, Mr Hedges? I sent mine back to the station with the uniformed sergeant and PC, so I'm looking for a lift."

Melpomene was about to offer the Riley, but Hedges said he indeed had his car with him, so started to walk off with Jimmy Manley. Then Mel called after them, "We don't know, of course, whether Latham and Stringer are actually at the chemists' shop at the moment – they didn't come to the inquest, and neither did Dr Jenkins – I wonder what's going on? Why don't Alex and I go to the doctor's surgery and see if we can find out what became of him this morning?"

Dr Jenkins' surgery was simply a room in his residence. At the front door were two bell-pushes, labelled 'Surgery' and 'Private', so Mel pressed the former. They could hear the bell ringing somewhere inside the house, but there was no response, so she pressed it again – again no response, so Mel tried the 'Private' one. This time the sound was more distant, apparently at the back of the house. After a minute or two, the door was opened by an elderly woman, who had obviously been crying, and was holding a handkerchief to her eyes.

"The Doctor is not available – if you need medical attention, Dr Billings is four houses along, in that direction, good day."

She started to shut the door, but Melpomene caught her sleeve and said, "We are here to see Dr Jenkins on important business, not for treatment. If he's in, could you ask him whether he'll see us – here is our card."

At this, the woman glanced at the card and burst into floods of tears, stood aside, motioned them into the house and shut the door. Then she drew herself up and said, "I am Mrs Jenkins – my husband is not able to talk to anyone – he is in a drunken stupor! He started drinking after a process-server delivered a summons to an inquest this morning, and has consumed the best part of a bottle of brandy. He takes in nothing that I say, and he is now unconscious. I have been bathing his face with cold water, but I suppose that it needs only time for him to recover – I have very little experience with intoxication!"

Mel took her arm and said, "I should make you a cup of tea, while my husband goes to see how the Doctor is – where is he now, and where is your kitchen?"

Mrs Jenkins told Alex where to go, and led Mel to the kitchen.

Chapter 20

When Alex went up the doctor's bedroom, he found him indeed completely insensible, lying on his back on the bed and snoring. Alex, with some difficulty, because he was fairly bulky, rolled him onto his side, stopping the snoring, and quietly went down to join the others.

"You were right, of course, Madam – he will wake up eventually with a splitting headache and a bad taste in the mouth, but otherwise recovered. As for his state of mind, I can say nothing, except that he has evidently taken the whole affair badly. I will inform the Coroner's office of the circumstances – but your husband will be obliged to attend the inquest when it is reconvened, under pain of substantial penalty if he fails to turn up – please convince him of this, Mrs Jenkins."

Melpomene added, "We must go now – will you be all right, or should I ask a neighbour to step in?"

"Oh, please don't – we need to preserve our professional reputation, you understand. I shall telephone my sister-in-law to come and sit with us until Leslie is himself again. Thank you for your concern, Mr and Mrs Crabbe!"

In the car, Mel asked, "Should we go to Latham and Sons' shop now, or simply wait until Jimmy lets us know what's happening?"

"I would like to go there as soon as possible, Mel, I'm keen to get to talk to Latham and the dispenser, Stringer, mainly about their drug suppliers, of course. I have assumed that these tablets are manufactured in a factory – the time when local chemists rolled their own pills is fast passing, probably completely gone by now. My guess is that the suppliers provide these tablets in bulk, and the dispensers simply count out the prescribed quantity into small bottles for the customers. Latham and Stringer will verify this, no doubt."

"But, Alex," said Melpomene, "if you are just wanting to find out about how drug supply is organized, this will distract the dispenser, Mr Stringer, from tackling the main question of how the wrong strength of Donnatal was given to Mrs Pratt-Smithers – if he is being devious it will give him an avenue to excuse himself. So why don't we go first to Timothy Whites' –

it's in Peckham High Street, too – and see if we can talk to the elderly dispenser with the goatee who originally upset the lady?"

Mel parked the Riley where they could see both Lathams' and Timothy Whites' shops, which were different in size, walked into the latter, and approached the counter, where a woman in a white coat was serving a customer. When she had finished, Alex said "Good afternoon, I wonder if we could speak to one of your dispensers, I'm afraid we don't know his name, but he is elderly, with a goatee, do you know who we mean?"

"Oh yes, Sir, that's Mr Kenworth, I know he's on duty now – we have three dispensers altogether and one or two of them are always on duty. If you would like to go and ring the little bell on the counter at the back of the shop, marked 'Prescriptions', someone will attend to you. I have to stay here and serve customers, otherwise I would take you myself."

They walked past displays of housewares, found the counter and rang the bell. A man with a goatee came out, and Alex addressed him, "Mr Kenworth? We have a couple of things we'd like to talk to you about, if you've got the time – here is our card, we are private detectives."

"I have already spoken to the police this morning," said Kenworth, "a Detective-Constable Thomson came and asked me about a prescription for Donnatal that I had refused to make up – are you talking about the same thing? I was very mortified and at the same time relieved to hear from him that my misgivings had been justified, since the poor lady has since met her end, possibly from taking those pills obtained elsewhere – he didn't say where."

"Yes, indeed, Mr Kenworth – but we wanted to ask about how such medicines are supplied to your shop – we know that big enterprises like Boots have their own arrangements and work directly with the manufacturers of pharmaceutical products – is it the same with Timothy Whites?"

"Well, yes and no. We do get some lines that are heavily in demand direct from factories – some even from firms on the continent – but for the most part we rely on wholesale dealers in England. That particular product, Donnatal, would come through Katzenberg's if we were to carry it, but in fact we don't – it is mainly within the province of hospitals rather than of local general practitioners."

Alex looked meaningfully at Melpomene, and said, "Thank you very much, Mr Kenworth. By the way, do you do much business with Katzenberg's – is it a reliable supplier?"

Kenworth gave a short dismissive laugh, "You've obviously been talking to other people! I have recommended to our branch manager, and to head office, that if we can possibly obtain goods elsewhere, we should! I have had several occasions here when orders from Katzenberg's have been mixed up, both as to quantities and to correctness of the product. When we are forced to get certain medicines from them, I always check and double-check the orders! I have reached the conclusion that they cut corners in an attempt to make more money, in particular by employing orders clerks that are not properly trained and up to the job!"

Alex went on, "You have been very helpful, Mr Kenworth – can I take up a little more of your time to check an assumption of mine? I have been guessing that pills and tablets come from the suppliers in bulk, and that you and your colleagues count them into the patients' small bottles according to prescriptions – is that so?"

"That's a good guess, Mr Crabbe, but there are exceptions for common medicines not requiring prescriptions, such as aspirins and antacids. These are sent by the manufacturers already in bottles or packets of a convenient size for most customers. So we get from the distributors cartons of several dozen bottles, which we put out on the open shelves. Prescription pills, like those Donnatals, come packed in tins, or in cartons lined with a damp-proof material."

"One further question, Mr Kenworth – in those cases, I suppose that the strength of the dose is listed on a label attached to that tin or carton, is that so?"

"You are putting your finger on a possible source of error, Mr Crabbe – I can see why you are a successful detective! Once the pills have been removed from the bulk container, then they become anonymous, save for some that have code letters impressed on the tablets themselves. My practice, shared by my colleagues – in this company, at any rate – is to count them into the final bottles for the customer directly from the tin or carton."

"We thank you most sincerely, Mr Kenworth – we are grateful that you took the time and trouble to tell us all this. Good day!"

Chapter 21

Melpomene said, "Now let's try Lathams – perhaps Jimmy will still be there, but that won't be any problem, will it?"

As it happened, as they were walking up to the shop, Jimmy Manley and the solicitor, Hedges, came out and stood talking on the pavement. When they saw Mel and Alex they beckoned them to join the conversation.

Talbot Hedges said, "Detective-Inspector Manley suggested that it would not be advisable for all of us to speak to the manager and the dispenser together – if it comes to a court case, the police and defence counsel would be on opposing sides, of course. So I have not found out very much yet."

Jimmy nodded and said, "I'm glad Mr Hedges took my point – but there is no reason why you two should not make your enquiries with Mr Hedges present – in fact it might make your task easier if that were to give them more confidence. One important point he made to me was about the source of the Donnatal pills – he will tell you as well, no doubt – he has given me the partly-used carton to take away and keep safely as evidence. So, I shall leave all three of you to it. Don't worry about giving me a lift, Talbot, I can just as soon go by tube – New Cross Gate station is not far away – and it will be good for me to have a bit of a walk and then sit still for a while and consolidate my notes!"

They pushed open the door and went into the shop, which had an air of past times about it, even to shelves of antique porcelain apothecary jars behind the counter, bearing names such as 'EXTR. DULCAM.', 'EMPL. de MINIO.' and 'NUX VOMICA.'

Two men, one in a suit, the other wearing a white coat, were standing at the back of the shop talking together. They looked up expectantly as the party entered, and the suited one said, "Detective-Inspector Manley mentioned that we might receive a visit from detectives, but, I must admit, I was expecting persons looking older and perhaps seedier than you – I assume you are, in fact, Mr and Mrs Crabbe? And I've known Talbot Hedges for a while, he represented us in a dispute with some wholesalers last year – I am Douglas Latham and this is my dispensing pharmacist, Mr Edwin Stringer."

They all shook hands, and Latham said, "We might be more private and comfortable talking in the dispensary, if you don't mind sitting on stools – this way, please."

Talbot Hedges was the first to speak, once everyone was seated.

"The Coroner's duty is to discover how Mrs Pratt-Smithers met her end, and whether any person or persons is culpable. If it should be the case that he does find anyone culpable, he will probably recommend that charges be laid. If either you, Mr Latham, or you, Mr Stringer, are charged, then I will represent you in any court proceedings that might follow, and engage a barrister on your behalf should that seem advisable. Any questions that I ask now are merely so that I can have an accurate view of the circumstances – I am not bound to offer your answers in evidence – so I hope you will feel free to be frank with me. Mr and Mrs Crabbe must speak for themselves."

"Thanks for that, Talbot," said Alex, "Melpomene and I are here to discover the facts, like the Coroner, but I must add that we both have wider interests, in the first instance, to do with the supply of pharmaceutical products to hospitals. We have been retained by a member of staff of a local hospital to investigate the causes of a number of instances of errors in delivering medicines and we are beginning to build our evidence. But, quite independently, Mrs Pratt-Smithers approached our agency, requesting us to investigate a script that Dr Jenkins wrote for her, which was queried by another dispensing pharmacist as inappropriate for her complaint. She is – was – an impulsive and opinionated lady, so before we had a chance to follow this up, she brought the script here – you know the rest."

Mr Stringer, the dispenser, wanted first to make a point, "Before we get to anything else, I must tell you that I have already explained to the Detective-Inspector that I dispensed those pills directly from a manufacturer's carton marked 'Donnatal, 3/4 grain', the dose prescribed. This was a safe dose, given the lady's age and size, so I was unconcerned, apart from wondering why the doctor had prescribed that medicine for anxiety and insomnia, I could have suggested several alternative remedies, but unfortunately we pharmacists are at the beck and call of the doctors."

Alex said "Can I take you up on a point you made earlier, Mr Latham. You said that Mr Hedges represented you earlier in a case about a wholesaler. As we've said, we are interested in the whole question of the supply of pharmaceuticals – could I ask what that dispute was about, and which wholesaler was involved?"

"Certainly, Mr Crabbe, the firm involved was Hathaway and Woodruff, and the dispute was about errors in the fulfilment of orders, with our contention being that substitutions of inferior or unsuitable products had been made, with no authority from us!"

"Very interesting!" said Alex, "Do you also deal with Katzenberg's? We have come across both of these firms already, in various contexts."

"We certainly do! The Donnatal tablets were ordered from them – and it looks increasingly likely that they have messed up that order, too! The only reason we placed it with them is that our preferred supplier – one that has hardly ever caused us any problems – was unable to supply Donnatal at the moment, and I was unwilling to suggest alternatives to the customer, given her intransigence! That drug is, I believe, manufactured only by a small number of firms in continental Europe – mainly Germany and Switzerland, and our main supplier, Carey and Donaldson, had found it difficult to acquire it – for what reason I do not know."

"So tell me more, Mr Latham."

"We have a long history of problems with Katzenberg's, Mr Crabbe, dating back about five or seven years when the company changed hands. It had long been merely a branch of a Swiss company, but was bought out at that time by a large local group, which had formerly specialized in industrial solvents for the paint and printing industries. In my opinion, they bit off more than they could properly chew! I found out much of this information in my searches for the case I mentioned before. We found also that Hathaway and Woodruff were another target of the same parent company that had been behind the Katzenberg acquisition."

"So – wheels within wheels!" exclaimed Melpomene, "Do you know the name of that parent company – is it based in England, or is it another Swiss firm?"

"Neither, Mrs Crabbe – it is Scottish – Dalgleish and McDonald is its name, based in Dumfries!"

Chapter 22

"Do they have a local office in London?" asked Alex, "Even though I love touring in Scotland, at this time of the year I would prefer to avoid long drives or train journeys, and I would rather like to talk to these people."

"I'm not sure, Mr Crabbe – we have no occasion to deal with them directly – but they would be listed in the telephone book, I should imagine – or Katzenberg's or Hathaway's would tell you."

"Thanks, anyway, Mr Latham, we'll look in the book. While we're here with Mr Stringer and yourself, we might take the opportunity to widen our net. You've mentioned two suppliers so far – do you depend on any others? We are particularly interested, of course, in those you have found to be deficient in any respect, or are difficult to deal with."

Edwin Stringer leant forward and said, "Our most reliable source, which has never given us anything but prompt and efficient service, is Hardcastle Brothers. This is an old family firm which Mr Latham's father – rest his soul – relied on for many years, even before I joined the business, which was before Mr Lathham – I've finally stopped calling him 'young Mr Latham' – took over."

"I'm still not that old, Edwin!" said Latham, "You're right – in the old days, you could sit with the reps over a cup of tea while you put in your orders – but now it's all business, business, business, with no time for anything else, so it's not surprising that mistakes get made. But Hardcastles, as you say, are still one of the best! How have you found Simpsons or Bradleys, Edwin? I haven't heard you complaining about them."

"I have no problem with either of them, Douglas, it's a pity that they are so specialized, so we only get a limited range from them, mainly of ointments, balms and ladies' necessities – not lines which turn over very fast for us, since Boots and Timothy Whites can afford to stock a more comprehensive range. The old style family chemist will soon join the dinosaurs, I'm afraid!"

Melpomene looked at Alex and said, "We thank you for this, gentlemen – it was good of you to spare us the time. No doubt we shall see you again when the Coroner reconvenes the inquest. Good day to you both, and to you, Mr Hedges."

As they left the shop and started to walk back to the car, Melpomene said "You know what, Alex – I'm starving! What shall we do about lunch? That looks like a possibility over the road, there – 'La Cucina Bella' – sounds suitably Italian."

Alex agreed, so they went over and pushed open the door, to encounter a mixture of aromas – wine, food and cigar-smoke – and a babble of excitable conversation. A waiter greeted them and led them to what might have been the only free table, just being vacated by two men with swarthy complexions wearing black silk shirts under their shiny striped suits. The waiter excused himself as he cleared the used plates and wine glasses away, returning almost at once to give them menus.

Mel had no difficulty in deciding on chicken cacciatori, while Alex more modestly went for a bowl of minestrone, and they were soon both tucking in while sipping the house chianti.

After a while, Mel said, "It's puzzling, but I've got the feeling that I know the man sitting to the right of the door with his back to the window – but I just can't recall his name nor where I've seen him. Have a discreet peep when you get a chance – he's wearing a navy blue blazer."

When Alex beckoned the waiter for coffee, he had a good long look, and then broke into a grin, saying, "I think I know where you saw him before – he's one of Jimmy's plain-clothes men – I remember him from when he and his mates came to take away the crooks who kidnapped Marie-Colette Huskisson after we'd caught them. I wonder what he's doing in this neck of the woods?"

Said Mel, "One certainly could get the feeling that the clientele here is very mixed – there are some hulking types here who could well be stand-over men, and there's a guy in the corner with a beautiful suit and a haircut to match who could easily be a gang boss from Chicago, as portrayed in that movie we saw 'Alias Jimmy Valentine'. When we get back to the office, I'll telephone Jimmy Manley and see what he thinks."

Melpomene had to wait a while, because when they got back after a half-hour journey slowed by road-works on the Embankment, there were a number of messages to deal with first.

"Your Mama rang again," said Marjorie, "but this time it sounds a little more than just wanting to chat – Lady Cynthia said something about an important letter that had arrived for you."

"I'll talk to her as soon as I've had a cup of tea," said Mel, "somehow my last cup of coffee at the café has left an after-taste."

When she spoke to her mother, Melpomene found her sounding a little anxious, "Shall I read this letter to you, dear, I'm a bit bothered because it isn't signed and has no return address – but it doesn't seem like a threat or anything like that. Here it is – the sender hasn't even got the spelling of your name right, '*Melpommy, I want you to know that there is no point in talking to hospital people if you really want to find out what is going on in the medication supply industry. However, the ones who really know are not likely to tell you anything unless you get a hold over them. I suggest that you need to bend the law a little! Birds in a cage sing the loudest! A concerned friend.*' What do you think of that?"

"My first question, Mama, is why was it sent to Woodhampton Castle Hotel? If they know I'm investigating medicine supplies, they must know the address of Crabbe and Crabbe, surely! I'm only in the telephone book under the addresses of our flat and the agency, so it makes me think that it might be someone who knew me before our wedding. Very puzzling!"

"To me, too!", said Lady Cynthia, "But I'm quite proud of myself that I took some precautions as soon as I saw there was no return address. I put some gloves on before I took the letter from the envelope, and I'm putting it into a clean envelope now. I was thinking of fingerprints, of course, was this the right thing to do?"

"Yes it was, darling Mama – I'm proud of you, too. I shan't be down for a while, so could you put it all into another big envelope and send it registered post to me at the office. I can get it to the police for testing, then. But he or she sounds careful, so maybe they've made sure not to get prints on it. Was it hand-written or typed?"

"Typed, Melpomene – but didn't I read somewhere that each typewriter has a distinct set of little variations in the way the letters line up and so on, so can be identified?" Mel laughed, "Go on reading those detective novels, Mama, you are picking up some useful information!"

Chapter 23

After chatting a little more with her mother, Mel told her she had better get on, but would telephone her later to give her all the rest of the news.

Then she asked Marjorie, "What were the other messages – did Jimmy Manley call?"

"Yes, Mel, he did, but maybe you should telephone Imogen or Dr Salmon first – I thought they both sounded a bit tense. Imogen will be at home by now, and Gordon can be reached at the emergency room, unless he's busy with an urgent admission, he said."

She tried Imogen first, to be told that when she had gone to the lab at University College that morning, she had found that someone had deliberately smashed all the Petri dishes that were being incubated from the previous day's sampling at Finchley Hospital. "Why anyone would want to do that, I have no idea! As far as I know, Vanessa and I have no rivals among the research staff or students, and, anyway, the loss of one day's data won't be more than a minor nuisance to the project. We asked around, but nobody had seen anyone acting suspiciously. The general opinion that it was done overnight – maybe by a trespasser, though the place is always closed up securely and watchmen patrol regularly – there is a lot of very expensive equipment around, but none of it seems to have been touched, according to the lab staff."

"Have the police been called?" asked Mel, to be told that the lab manager had not considered it worthwhile, even though on other occasions he had been quick to follow up incidents of theft or damage. "I'm about to telephone Gordon Salmon," said Mel, "I'll see if he has any ideas, though it's not really relevant to him – the only connection is Finchley Hospital. If I find out anything, of course I'll let you know."

She tried Gordon next, but was told that he was attending to a man who had walked through the glass doors of a department store without opening them. The woman who answered the telephone promised to pass on the message as soon as Dr Salmon had finished picking pieces of glass out of the man's face and arms.

Mel telephoned Jimmy Manley next, who answered the telephone immediately, and suggested that Alex listen in to the call on the spare earpiece, as he had something of great interest to tell them both.

"One of my men was keeping his eye on a bunch of people we suspect have been running a protection racket in shops and other businesses in the Peckham area. He tells me he was surprised to see you two at lunchtime in a café that we have worked out is a meeting-place for these crooks, and wondered whether you might have been on a similar mission. He was very impressed with his previous encounter with you!"

"No, no!" said Mel, "We have enough to cope with at the moment!"

"Well, he was saying that he saw you going into Lathams' chemist shop earlier, another surprise, since we have being keeping surveillance there for the last week or so. He didn't see you come out, because he handed over to another watcher while he went to grab something to eat – and then you turned up at that very café!"

"Oh, Jimmy, this is getting very interesting indeed! Why are you watching Lathams? Mr Latham and his dispenser, Mr Stringer, seemed very open and cooperative to us – Alex is making enquiries about some dubious pharmaceutical suppliers, by the way – so, if it's not a secret, can you let us know what is going on with you and your boys?"

"I'll tell you, Mel – and Alex if you're still listening – we had simply picked out Lathams as a likely target for protection racketeers, who have already brought their New York or Chicago tactics into Peckham and some other areas. We hoped to catch some of them in the act – a few days ago they cornered the elderly owner of a tobacconist's a few doors away from Lathams and, as we say, 'demanded money with menaces', threatening to ruin him unless he gave them a weekly fee for 'protecting his business against robbers'. Mr Higgins, the owner, is a plucky old geezer, and told them in no uncertain terms to 'sling their hook'! Two night later a brick was thrown through the shop window, wrapped in a further threatening demand. There have been similar incidents around the area."

Melpomene said, "Oh, Jimmy, I hope we haven't spoilt things for you – it hardly seems likely that our enquiries have anything to do with these gangsters, does it? Anyway, we now understand what your man was doing there! Give him my regards when you speak to him next! Did you want to tell us anything else? – no – well, see you later, Jimmy."

Alex agreed that this was all very interesting, "I'll try Gordon Salmon again – maybe he has uncovered a further criminal enterprise! If it goes on spreading like this, we'll have to take on extra staff!"

Doctor Salmon had finished patching up his patient and told Alex – Mel listening on the extension this time – that he thought he had stumbled onto another sort of shenanigans in the hospital.

"I can only talk to you for a moment, as I've got another victim to attend to! While I was fixing the glass door man – luckily nothing had got into his eyes, or it would have been serious rather than merely painful – another patient was brought in by the ambulance men on a stretcher. My young assistant had a quick look at him, as my hands were full, and had him taken to theatre to be prepped for an operation to remove a bullet from the shoulder! – I hope he wasn't shot by you, Mel, only kidding! I'm going up there now – it might be a good idea for one or both of you to come and see whether you can find out what happened to him – he was conscious and cursing when I saw him, but he will probably need a general for the surgery. We shall be in Theatre B, the door people will direct you. That theatre has viewing windows, so you'll be able to watch me at work if you want!"

"See you soon, Gordon – save the bullet for us!"

After a quick explanation to Marjorie and Winnie the two headed off to Finchley Hospital, and were soon settling into the observation seats for Theatre B, along with a couple of young eager students.

Apparently they had not missed the exciting parts – Gordon and the theatre sister, masked and gowned, were discussing tactics, while the anaesthetist was making his preparations on the patient.

Then sister drew aside the drapes and started swabbing the area round the wounded shoulder for Gordon to get to work.

Mel and Alex – and the students – were fascinated for the next hour or so, until Gordon stitched up the incision and stood back, proudly displaying a bowl containing the bullet!

Chapter 24

Mel and Alex went down and met Gordon outside the theatre, as he was throwing his discarded gown and mask into a laundry bin. He handed Alex a sealed test-tube containing the bullet, saying that Jimmy and his contacts would no doubt be able to check it out. "We've had the victim taken to a locked ward, with a policeman in attendance, who will interrogate him when he wakes up."

Then he took them into a vacant treatment room and said, "Finally, I can get round to telling you what I telephoned about before – sorry about that, but an A and E surgeon's life can get very busy sometimes! We have had almost an epidemic here, over the last week or two. Not an outbreak of disease, really, but an unusually large number of admissions of people with stomach cramps – a lot of schoolchildren, but a few adults, too. After the first few, Matron Stevenson realised there was a pattern developing, so she took a senior nurse off ward duties to put together a report, with instructions to visit homes where necessary and get hold of any information that might have any bearing on this. She also telephoned her opposite numbers at some of the nearby hospitals, but it seems that Finchley is the only place where this has been happening."

"What made you think of us, Gordon?" asked Melpomene, "We're no experts on medical matters, are we!"

"Maybe not, Melpomene, but you are experienced in making sense out of masses of information. My idea was that you should see what Sister Eunice Makepeace has been able to gather so far, and work with her to see whether you can come up with a probable cause for all these cases. Nothing obvious has emerged so far, at least nothing that Eunice or Matron or I can spot. Are you game, Mel?"

"Of course, Gordon!" said Mel with alacrity, "Do these cramps persist for long – do you have to keep people in, or do you send them home after checking them out? I wonder how many sufferers simply go to their family doctor, or treat their children themselves with popular remedies like Milk of Magnesia, Andrews or Eno. This might mean that we can only pick up a small fraction of the cases. I suppose the hospital would have addresses and telephone numbers for most of the local doctors

– it might be worth conducting a telephone survey, don't you think? We could get our Winnie or Marjorie to do this."

Gordon seemed very keen, "I knew you would be the right person to ask, Mel – go and talk to Matron about getting a list of doctors, unless you're worried about breaking your cover."

"No problem, Gordon – I can still be Henrietta Musgrave, just doing a different kind of research. I'll clear this with Imogen and Vanessa, of course. Have you formed any ideas about possible causes yet? You said it didn't look like a disease, didn't you? Could it be poisoning? Oh – mentioning Imogen and Vanessa reminds me – did you hear that their last batch of Petri dishes, incubating a set of swabs collected here a day or two ago, was deliberately destroyed?"

Alex broke in at this point, "I've been wondering whether that was an attempt at a cover-up. Your average crook-in-the-street wouldn't understand what those bacterial cultures could reveal, so maybe some crime boss was worried that it would uncover whatever his gang might be doing that has caused the outbreak of cramps."

"And that raises questions of motive," said Melpomene, "I can understand the use of threats of violence to shop-keepers as a way of extorting money – but how could poisoning a whole district be an effective strategy for raising funds for a criminal organization? And I'm still wondering how it could have been done – if it really is poisoning."

"Perhaps Eunice has found out something, Mel," said Gordon, "we made an arrangement that she would come and report to me at the end of every working day – official hospital hours that is – I quite often have to work through into the evening. We meet in the staff common-room – shall we go?"

Gordon introduced Sister Eunice Makepeace, who was wearing plain clothes and explained, "The first day I went out in my nursing uniform, but people assumed I was available for medical advice. I didn't really mind – I think I helped one or two families – but it tended to slow me down, so since then I've just been wearing a dress and raincoat. I started with a household who had brought in a girl of about eleven, one of the first cases we saw at the hospital. She has recovered well and was already at school when I visited, but her Mum told me how the cramps had started just after breakfast one morning, so the child was kept at home. By lunchtime she was in intense pain, so she was brought in here and examined. She was not running a temperature, so the staff in outpatients gave her something, antacid her Mum thought, and after she had laid down for a while, she said she felt well enough to go home."

"So," asked Mel, "did you find many cases of this sort – were you working from a list, or what?"

"I had a list that Matron gave me, but I could see that the cases were scattered about, so I decided just to work house-to-house, and see what this would bring. And it turned out it was a good decision! I've made my own list, and in the evenings I've been comparing the two. My list is much more comprehensive, because not everyone came to the hospital – some went to their doctor – but mostly they treated the cramps at home with whatever they had to hand, Milk of Magnesia, Andrews Liver Salts, California Syrup of Figs, hot water bottles applied to the tummy, and so on."

"Have you detected any common features in the cases?", asked Mel.

"Yes indeed. The onset of the cramps was in most cases about half an hour to an hour after breakfast – and they had all had milk in one form or another – on their cornflakes or porridge, or just to drink, on its own or with cocoa or tea. I'm fairly confident that it is the milk that we need to look at. I brought away some samples from houses where the cramps had started that morning and gave them to the pathologists for testing, but I haven't heard anything yet. I took the names and addresses of everyone I visited, and noted what had happened."

"Were there any places you visited where milk had been taken with no ill-effects?", Alex asked, "I'm beginning to think that there is one item you have left off – the name of the dairy that supplied the milk."

At this, Eunice became very distressed, saying, "Oh, how could I? What a silly mistake! I'm so sorry – I'll go back tomorrow and find out!"

"No need!" said Alex, "we can get that information a much better way – the dairies must have customer lists. I expect the delivery men soon get to know their round, and don't have to refer to their list, but I bet the companies don't rely on that, in case a milkman leaves the firm, or goes on holiday!"

Chapter 25

Alex and Melpomene said goodbye to Gordon Salmon and Eunice Makepeace, Mel saying that she would come to the hospital the next day to see whether the pathologists had any results on the milk testing and also to find out what the police had done with the shooting victim.

Alex took the wheel of the Riley on the way home, while Mel went into a brown study. When they were nearly at the flat, she clapped her hands and exclaimed, "Of course – it's the dairy company that's the target – not the customers! I'll explain once we've had a cup of tea, Alex!"

When Caroline greeted them, Mel said "Which milkman do we get our milk from, Caroline? I mean which dairy – I suppose it's you who pays the bill, isn't it?"

"At home, here, it's Watson's Pasteurized Milk – the milkman calls in of a Friday to collect the money – you'll have to ask Marjorie who delivers to the office, or maybe they pick their milk up from the shop."

Over her usual cup of Lapsang Souchong, taken black as always, Melpomene told them her idea, "This outbreak of stomach cramps is probably the first step in a campaign by some criminal organization to extort money from milk companies. They'll say that this time it was simply stomach cramps that were easily treated – next time it will be something more deadly! What do you say, Alex, am I barking up a gum-tree?"

"Sounds good, my darling! Possibly it's the same mob that has been working the protection racket in Peckham. Tomorrow when you're at the hospital, ask Eunice whether she has found out which dairy – or dairies – delivered the suspect milk. Then you can see what the hospital pathologist, Dr Aitcheson, has found out, if anything. Meanwhile, I shall go and talk to Jimmy Manley – I need to tell him what I've been doing with the pharmaceutical supplies companies, as well as asking him about our stand-over friends. It would be too neat if it were to transpire that the shot guy from yesterday had anything to do with any of this!"

After dinner, a rolled roast with baked vegetables, Mel and Alex decided not to talk shop any more, but listen to a concert broadcast by the British Broadcasting Company from Queen's Hall, in which Beatrice Harrison was to perform the new Delius cello concerto.

"Is this the same lady who plays the cello in her garden with nightingale accompaniment?", asked Alex after the concert. "Yes, that's right," said Melpomene, "but some people are saying that it's not a real nightingale at all, but someone whistling!"

After the concert, Mel was about to switch off the wireless, but Alex reminded her that it was nearly time for the nine o'clock news. After the six pips of the time signal, the news was announced. The first items were of little interest, but then the newsreader said, "*There was a sensational incident in a shop in Moorgate earlier today, in which an elderly pawnbroker was shot dead. Police are releasing few details, but it is believed that a man was demanding money, when the shop-keeper, Mr Jacobson, struck at him with an iron bar that he was known to keep behind the counter for self-defence. There were traces of blood and hair on the bar, which has been taken away by the police for closer examination. A Mrs Hilda Wheeler, who owns the sweet-shop next door, said that Mr Jacobsen was usually a very quiet and kind man. As the assailant ran out of the shop, a passer-by tried to detain him, but was shot in the shoulder. The shooter escaped through the crowds on the footpath and the shot man was taken away by ambulance. On the London Stock Market today ...*"

Mel switched off the set and said, "That must be the man who Gordon patched up today! I'm very tempted to telephone Jimmy straight away, but it's getting a bit late, even for a policeman!"

"That sounds as though the stand-over gangs are moving into new areas, Mel," said Alex, "though there might be no connection. If they are also behind the milk business then it looks as though we're up against yet another criminal organization with tentacles that are spreading wider and wider! Start carrying your pistol at all times, my darling – I shall certainly do the same!"

Melpomene nodded, and went on, "It would be stretching things to suggest that they are also connected with your pharmaceutical people, I suppose, Alex. But who knows?"

74

The next morning they were both at the office so early that they beat Marjorie in, though Winnie was there already.

"What's up, Mel and Alex? You look as though you have the scent in your nostrils!"

"Have we got the morning papers yet?", asked Mel. "Marjorie usually picks them up when she gets the milk and jam tarts," replied Winnie, "she should be in very soon."

Marjorie arrived almost as Winnie was speaking, and Melpomene almost snatched 'The Trumpet' from her hands. There on the front page, was the story she was looking for.

But the only extra detail that the BBC had not given was that the injured man, Mr Neville Butler, had made a good recovery, had been collected by his wife and gone home in plaster and a sling. Reporters had tried to interview him, but he had told them in no uncertain terms that he would give his full story to the police first.

Alex had meanwhile been perusing 'The Times', but that carried even less detail, befitting a paper with a more conservative image to maintain.

"All right, Mel," he said, "let's see what more Jimmy has to tell us! Please get him for us, Winnie – then you two can read the papers and see what we are on about!"

Disappointingly, Jimmy Manley was not at Mile End Road police station, but his assistant, Detective-Constable Cecil Thomson, said that Jimmy had told him he would be getting in touch with them as soon as he could. "He was off interviewing Mr Butler at his home – it turns out he is a local dentist and is well respected in the district – I suppose that's why the Finchley police let him go home so soon."

"Thanks, Cec – can't be helped, we shall just have to contain ourselves. Any developments in the other stand-over cases?"

"No, Alex. Nobody came near Lathams, and we've been maintaining a round-the-clock watch. Personally, I think we should try somewhere else – or take an altogether different approach. I'll talk to Jimmy about it when he's back in the station."

"We'll see you later maybe – I have plans to approach some of the local dairies today about this stomach cramps business – I assume Gordon Salmon has mentioned it to Jimmy and you?"

75

Chapter 26

Melpomene said, "I'm off to the hospital now, Alex. I expect you'll need the car if you are going to visit dairy companies, so I'll just go by tube."

"No need, Mel, I'll come with you first – I need to talk to Eunice some more, anyway. We'll pop into Mrs Jenkins' on the way to the car and see who supplies milk for her shop – we always buy it from her and we've had no stomach problems with it here in the office, so we might be able to eliminate another firm straight away – we have already found out that Watson's Pasteurized Milk is off the suspect list."

At the shop, Mrs Jenkins told them that she too got her milk from Watsons – so that they had got no further with their elimination. They parked at the hospital and went looking for Eunice. At the front desk, the receptionist informed them that all staff members checked in and wrote their time of arrival in a ledger kept next to the staff entrance, so they went and discovered that Sister Makepeace had arrived and had told the clerk that she would be in Willett Ward initially and would be going out on her rounds later.

They found their way to the ward and discovered Eunice at her desk in the ward office. "Some progress with the dairies!", she announced, "I remembered that one of the families I visited lived over a hardware shop, whose name I remembered, so I rang them up and asked which dairy supplied that neighbourhood. The proprietor didn't know, but I heard him call out to someone to ask, and then he told me that it was Bloomfields Speedy Milk. I've certainly seen their milk-floats around."

"Right!" said Alex, "That's who I shall visit first. Have you got a telephone book here, Eunice? I'll find their address and call there in person – there are too many problems with trying to make enquiries over the telephone. Ah, I see their head office is in Hackney, so I'll need the Riley. Before I rush off, have you had any results from Dr Aitcheson about his analysis of the milk?"

"No, Alex, I was about to walk up there – do you two want to come? I know Dr Aitcheson quite well, so I don't mind asking him."

"We've met him, too!" said Mel, "When he was doing a PM on a client of ours. We went to her inquest, and he reported the cause of death. The inquest had to be adjourned, so we shan't know the Coroner's verdict until it's reconvened – I'm inclined to think it was murder, but it will probably come out as death by misadventure!"

Dr Aitcheson was at his desk in the pathology department, but stood up to shake Alex and Mel's hands when he recognized them.

"And Sister Makepeace, too!" he said, "How can I help you – oh, I know, it's about the milk. This was exceedingly interesting, and it took me a while to discover the adulterant – but I found it after a number of tests – it turned out to be borax. This is not hard to get hold of, because it is used, for example, in household cleaning products. It is inconceivable to me, however, that so many cases could be the result of inadvertent actions – I believe that there must have been deliberate malicious acts!"

Alex said, "I'm about to go and make enquiries at the Bloomfields' plant in Hackney, Dr Aitcheson, but I will not be too quick to mention your name, nor that of this hospital. I shall be fairly naïve, saying that some of their customers have become concerned that it might be the milk giving their children stomach cramps, and did they have anything to say. Depending on the reaction I get, if any, I might then proceed with more searching questions."

Alex parked outside the factory at Hackney, which consisted mainly of a yard, with stables for a dozen horses and the same number of milk floats, as well as two large tanker lorries. The floats were all empty, and the loading dock held only a few empty milk-bottle crates. To one side were some outside iron stairs, leading up to a couple of floors above the loading dock, so Alex asked a man attending to the horses if he could go up, as he wanted to talk to the manager.

"Yes, sir, go on up. Anyone up there will tell you where Mr Stanley has his office. I know he's in, because he was talking to me only a few minutes ago. Are you from the council? He said that there had been complaints – what about I couldn't say, sir."

A woman showed Alex into Mr Stanley's office, and the manager, a worried-looking thinnish man, with greying hair and glasses, looked up enquiringly. Alex quickly made up his mind to adopt a vague role, saying, "My name is Alan Robertson, Mr Stanley – I hope I'm not interrupting your work, but some of the residents in my ward have been a little worried about some minor health matters that they thought might have had something to do with the milk delivered to their homes. I just wanted to get your assurance that you were taking every precaution to maintain hygiene and high quality."

"I can certainly put your mind to rest over those matters, Mr Robertson. Please take a seat and I will explain every stage our milk passes through on its way from the milking shed in the country to the customers' front step."

Alex had the impression that he was just about to be presented with a well-rehearsed speech, suitable for a local Chamber of Commerce or for many a school speech night. He settled back, put his finger-tips together, and looked ready to be enthralled.

Stanley proceed to describe the entire journey of a pint of milk, omitting no step from the udder to the breakfast bowl. He finished almost triumphantly and asked whether Alex had any questions, obviously expecting nothing of any weight.

Alex said, "Merely some minor points of detail, Mr Stanley. I gather that the tankers that convey the milk from the farm to the railway wagons, those wagons, and the tanker-trucks that bring it to your rail siding here are all meticulously cleaned before each and every trip – am I right?"

"You certainly are, Mr Robertson, they are steam-cleaned at each point. Here at the depôt we steam-clean the tankers after they are emptied into our holding tanks and before they are taken back to the main railway line, then the same procedure is used between the farms and our depôt at the LNER main-line station in Suffolk. We have our own installation there, which deals with the trucks going to the farms and also scalds out the rail wagons before they are filled. I assure you that we are scrupulous about this!"

"So we have finally brought the milk safely to your bottling plant – which is here, I suppose."

"Yes, that's right. The milk never stays more than a few hours in our holding tanks here, which are steam-cleaned before they are filled, before a refrigeration plant cools them and the milk coming from the railway wagons. They stay like that overnight, so the milk is quite cool before it is bottled."

Chapter 27

"Tell me, Mr Stanley – are the bottles filled by machinery or by hand?"

"Oh, although we're very modern here, Mr Robertson, we have not yet been able to make the bottle filling completely automatic. Let me show you – it's not easy to explain – please come with me. Oh, Joyce, I'm taking this gentleman to the bottling shop – if there are any urgent telephone calls, come and get me."

They went down some stairs to a long room, with high double doors at the back and several large tanks. "This is on the level of the railway siding," said Stanley, "we're built on a slope, which makes this possible. Near the doors is the boiler for steam-cleaning the railway wagons when they're emptied. If you put your hand on one of these holding tanks, you'll find they are refrigerated. The cooling plant is on the ground floor, along with the bottling lines."

"You can see what happens," went on Stanley, as they went down another level and stopped in front of a series of conveyor belts, each carrying a row of milk bottles, but not moving. There was only one workman there, doing some tidying-up, by the look of things.

The manager's account continued, "Starting at about five o'clock in the morning, clean bottles move steadily past each worker, seated on these stools. He or she – they are mostly women – takes a bottle and positions it under the spout, and presses a foot pedal to turn on the milk, which flows through pipes from the holding tanks on the floor above. When the bottle is full, she takes one of these cardboard discs and inserts it into the top of the bottle – there is a shoulder in the neck to position the disc, as you see, and puts the full bottle back on the belt. They get very quick and dextrous at this after a while! There is a man at the end of each belt to put the full bottles into the crates, and pile them up for the milk delivery men to take and load onto their horse-floats."

"Over here are the bottle-washing tanks and the steam cabinets where the bottles are sterilised. We try to reuse as many bottles as possible, but we rely on the customers to put them out for collection by the milkmen and we inevitably lose a proportion, so we are always needing new bottles. Whether they are new from the glass-works or washed ones being reused, they are all steam-sterilised before refilling."

Alex pondered for a moment, then said, "Thank you very much for showing me all this, Mr Stanley. I have something rather important to tell you, so can we go back up to your office, please?"

Back in the office, Stanley asked for tea to be brought, and then said, "Thank you, Joyce. Please do not disturb us for while. Now, Mr Robertson, what was it?"

"I'll be frank with you now, Mr Stanley. I intentionally gave you the impression that I am from the local council – I am not, neither is my name Alan Robertson – I am a private investigator, Alex Crabbe, and I'm working with the police. Your dairy has been the target of a criminal assault, in preparation, we think, for a major attempt at extortion. I believe you are blameless in this – you have been frank and open with me, with no hint of any cover-up. Fortunately this has so far caused only comparatively minor inconvenience to a number of your customers – painful but temporary stomach cramps. Tell me, Mr Stanley, have you had any complaints about your milk?"

Stanley was obviously shaken by all this, paling and shaking his head distractedly. "No, Mr Crabbe, I've heard nothing, I assure you!"

"I'm glad to hear that, Mr Stanley. We ourselves have only recently discovered the link between these symptoms and your milk, so it seems that none of your customers have put two and two together yet. The fact is that analysis has shown that at least one of your batches of milk over the last couple of days has been adulterated with borax! My guess is that someone sneaked in during the night, probably by way of the doors that give onto the railway siding, and poured a strong borax solution into one or more of your holding tanks."

"So what are they trying to do, these criminals? What profit can this possibly be for them?"

"We believe that this is just a first step. You should expect to receive a threatening message very soon, possibly by letter or telephone call, saying that, unless you pay out some considerable sum of money, your customers will be harmed further, or at least they will be convinced that your milk is dangerous, so destroying your business! This approach bears a resemblance to the stand-over tactics that have been used with shopkeepers, who have been forced to pay 'protection money' to keep their businesses from being damaged. This evil trade has been known for some time in places like Chicago and New York, and it is evidently now spreading to London!"

"So, what should I do if I receive such a threat – ignore it, or what?"

"You should immediately telephone Detective-Inspector Manley at Mile End Road police station – here is his number. If you can't speak to him right away just leave a message – and you could telephone me as well – I'll write my numbers, office and home, down for you too. Try not to handle any letter any more than you have to – slip it and its envelope into a big envelope or folder to give to Jimmy Manley, so he can have it tested for fingerprints. If the threat is by telephone, stall by saying you need proof, or put him or her off in any way that seems appropriate at the time. I doubt he will give you his number!"

"Should I keep this all to myself, Mr Crabbe? My secretary, Joyce, opens all my mail and takes my telephone calls. She is very trustworthy!"

"By all means put her in the picture, but ask her not to talk about it. I have no evidence that any of your employees are complicit with the crooks, but there is no point in taking any chances."

Alex rose and took his leave, shaking hands with Mr Stanley, who introduced him to Joyce as he left the office.

He went down the outside iron stairs and saw that grooms were feeding and otherwise attending to the horses in the stables. He decided to drive back to the office, rather than going straight home, so he could put Marjorie and Winnie into the picture.

Melpomene had not come back to the office, he was told, but had telephoned in case there had been any messages. He told the secretaries of his exploits at the dairy and asked Winnie to peruse all the London papers, including the evening editions, carefully, for any stories that might mention problems with milk.

Chapter 28

Before Alex left to go home, he asked whether they had heard from Jimmy Manley.

"Yes, Alex," said Marjorie, "but only to let us know that he had got some useful information from Neville Butler, the man who was shot outside the pawn-brokers. He said he would come to the office first thing tomorrow and tell you the whole story."

Melpomene had already got home when Alex arrived and had plenty to say, so he told her to go ahead and he would relate his experiences at the dairy to her afterwards.

"Vanessa and Imogen certainly have their wits about them!" Mel exclaimed, "Even though the lab manager at University College had thought it unnecessary to call the police in when the damaged Petri dishes had been discovered, Vanessa telephoned the local police station, and they sent a Detective-Constable round. He was young and keen, and called in a finger-print specialist, who dusted the incubating cabinet and lifted several prints from it with sticky tape, and also took away a few of the Petri dishes that had not been completely shattered. He took Vanessa's and Imogen's prints, and those of the regular lab technician, for comparison purposes, and said he would let them know what results he could come up with. Imogen told him that Jimmy Manley would be interested, too, and he said that he had worked with Jimmy and Cec Thomson before and would certainly talk to them. He asked the lab staff if anyone had seen any strangers lurking around, but they simply said that the building was always thronged with students, so who could tell which of them were strangers."

"Did they say when they might get these results, Mel?"

"No, but Jimmy telephoned and said that he would keep a watching brief for us. He also said he had made some progress with the bullets retrieved from Mr Jacobson, the murdered pawnbroker, and from Neville Butler. Not surprisingly, the tests showed that both had been fired from the same pistol – not a Luger this time, but a Smith and Wesson 38-calibre revolver."

"He was going to interview Mr Butler, wasn't he? Did he get anything of value from him?"

"Yes, Alex – Butler got a good look at the man who shot him. He told Jimmy that time seemed to stop as the revolver was being levelled at him and he now has an indelible impression in his mind of the man snarling at him as he tried to bar his escape! What is more, Alex – this is quite funny – being a dentist, he noticed that the crook had gold fillings in his front teeth, which he swears he will recognize if he ever sets eyes on him again!"

"What about fingerprints at the pawnbrokers, Mel? Did Jimmy say whether they had done any good there? I guess that the crook didn't have to touch very much there except the door – and that would be covered with prints from all the people going in and out all day. But they said something on the BBC news about an iron bar with blood and hair on it – did Jimmy mention this?"

"Yes, it's at the police lab now, but no results have reached Jimmy yet. He's not sure whether the reported blood and hair were from the assailant or not."

"My word, Mel, there is wealth of possible evidence here – I wonder whether anything useful will come from any of it – maybe it will become relevant, for identification purposes, if the police can ever pick up this gunman, but it really doesn't help us to find him."

He told Melpomene of his experiences at the dairy – she was pleased that he had been able to disclose his true identity, "We could get ourselves in all sorts of knots with our various *noms de guerre*! Is it worth getting Jimmy's fingerprint men to cast their eyes over the holding tanks at Bloomfield's, or do you think that's a vain hope? Did you notice what sort of lids the tanks have – would it have needed the crook to handle them to put in the borax solution?"

"As I recall, Mel, there was some sort of a hinged flap. I could ring up Stanley in the morning, but by that time they will have taken another delivery from the railway – no, enough is enough, I think we'll skip it this time, my dear!"

After dinner, which was a cold veal-and-ham pie with salad – Mrs M explaining, but without rancour, that she "couldn't put on a proper cooked dinner when I don't know when and if you two will be coming home!" – Melpomene announced, "As you say, enough is enough for one day – one crossword and I'm off to bed. What time is it?"

"Five to nine – let's see if the BBC has any exciting news, just for us!" Alex turned on the wireless to give it time to warm up and the announcer gave his usual introduction after the time signal, but he provided nothing of any interest until the very end of the bulletin, when he read, "*Finally, an item from the West End. A crowd, which had gathered in Leicester Square to see Miss Gracie Fields arrive in an open carriage for the opening night of her new musical play at the Alhambra Theatre, was thrown into uproar when a young woman fell under the horses' hooves while attempting to cross the road. She was helped by bystanders and taken to hospital by ambulance, but her injuries were not thought to be serious. That is the end of the News.*"

Mel and Alex thought no more about it, had their usual cups of chocolate and went to bed. But the next morning, while they were having breakfast, the telephone rang. It was Gordon Salmon, who told Mel, "I've just been checking on a young woman who was brought in last night after being run over by a horse. I fixed her up then – she had contusions and a cracked rib, which will all heal by themselves, but I had her kept in overnight because she was considerably shocked. When I spoke to her just now, as she was preparing to leave, she told me something that was very interesting to me and might also be of direct interest to you. I had to let her go home, but you might want to go and talk to her, because she swears she was pushed under the horse by a nasty-looking man with a mouthful of gold teeth! I got her to give me her name and address, have you got something to write on? She is called Miriam Schweitzer."

Mel passed on this conversation to Alex, saying, "Gordon doesn't forget much – I suppose it comes with his profession – so Neville Butler must have told him about the teeth after he had dug the bullet out of his shoulder and Gordon has put two and two together – I hope that they add up to four! Shall we go together to see this woman, Alex?"

The address was not very far, so they were there in less than fifteen minutes, pulling up outside a row of shops, as usual having flats above them. There was a doorway between a jewellers' shop and a beauty parlour, with the usual array of bell-pushes. Alex pushed the one labelled 'Schweitzer' and a disembodied female voice asked his name and business.

"Melpomene and Alex Crabbe – we're private investigators working with the police. Doctor Salmon at the hospital gave us your name – can we have a word?"

Chapter 29

The voice said, "Glad to meet you. I'm coming down – it'll take me a while. You'll find out why when you see me."

There was indeed at least a five minutes' wait before the door was opened and a woman stood there beckoning them in. She was walking with a stick, both legs were heavily bandaged and she was wearing a dressing-gown and slippers.

"Good morning, Mr and Mrs Crabbe, I'm Miriam Schweitzer. Dr Salmon told me he would get in touch with you. Please go on up – you'll see the door to the first-floor flat is open, so just go on in and I'll join you in a while!"

When she arrived, she took them into a sitting-room and asked them to sit, before lowering herself somewhat painfully to a settee.

"Would you like tea or coffee? I'm afraid you will have to make it yourselves – the kitchen is through there, and there are biscuits, too. I'm all right for the moment, my father made me breakfast and a pot of tea before he went down to open up the shop. Once you're settled, I'll relate you my sorry story!"

Mel went into the kitchen and made a pot of English Breakfast tea. There were lemons and a pot of honey on the table, so she put these, cups and saucers and tea-glasses and the pot, onto a tray and carried it into the room and set it down on the coffee table by the settee.

"Tell me how you like your tea," she asked, "I'm going to take mine continental-style with lemon and honey for a change!"

When they were all provided with teas and biscuits, Miriam began, "This whole saga goes back a day or two – my father and I were in the shop and had just sold a male customer a nice pair of ear-rings – for his fiancée, he said. After he left, in swaggered this heavy-set man – I didn't like the look of him and I was right, because he started to bully my father, telling him that a jewelry shop needed some special protection against thieves and that he and his associates could provide this for a fee – and then he quoted a weekly amount that would have amounted to nearly a quarter of our usual takings."

"Oh, yes!" said Alex, "We have heard that this despicable American practice is creeping into London, and we are already following up some enquiries."

"I know something about this," said Miriam, "a dear acquaintance of ours, Mr Jacobson, was murdered only a few days ago – we went to his funeral at the Golders Green crematorium as soon as his body was released by the police. Anyway, even knowing about that, my father, who is a very stubborn man, yelled at this crook to go away, saying they would never get anything from us! At this, the villain said 'Watch out, old man – don't forget that we know about your daughter, too!' and stormed out."

"If it was the same man who murdered Mr Jacobson, you're lucky your father didn't approach him, or he might have used his revolver again!" said Melpomene, "He is obviously a very violent and impulsive person!"

"So I was to find out last night!" said Miriam, "I was going with my friend Judith to the pictures, when we saw a big crowd gathering outside the Alhambra – we were not headed there, but we stopped and someone told us they were waiting for Gracie Fields to arrive. Then, up she drove in an open carriage drawn by four white horses. We were all cheering and waving, and then I noticed that same man sidling along the edge of the street towards us. He was looking at me, and laughing in a sinister way, opening his mouth and showing two rows of gold teeth, flashing in the glare of the floodlights there. And then, to my great shock, he grabbed me by the arm and threw me under the horses' hooves! I must have passed out, because the next thing I knew was being loaded on a stretcher and put into an ambulance."

"What horror!" said Mel, "But it could have been worse, given what he did to poor Mr Jacobson. I imagine you would have no difficulty in identifying him again, if only he could be nabbed by the police, but he will probably lie low now for a while. Your father must be very brave to open the shop so soon after that! Do you know whether he has taken any extra precautions?"

"The police were going to come this morning to talk to him about that," said Miriam, "but I haven't yet heard what was discussed. I was going to hobble down there later on to see what they said – Dad won't leave the shop until closing time, of course. I usually come up and make lunch and then take it down and eat it with him if there are no customers."

"I suppose someone from the police interviewed you at the hospital," said Alex, "did they say whether they had found out any more about this thug? We haven't had a chance yet to talk to our police contacts – we're certainly going to as soon as we can. Have you thought of anything else that you noticed about him, either when he came to the shop or last night? Clothing, hair, anything particular to look for?"

"Come to think of it, now, there was something, apart from the gold teeth, which are in any case rather distinctive themselves. He was of medium height, I'd suppose you would say, but he was walking sort of hunched up – he reminded me of a tall person avoiding knocking his head on a doorway, or something like that. Maybe he lives somewhere with a low ceiling. Apart from that he was pretty ordinary, dressed in trousers and a coat that didn't match – but that's not unusual these days. My Dad and people his age tend to wear suits, but that's getting a bit old-fashioned now. Oh – I see you have a suit on, Alex, so I take that remark back!"

Alex and Mel thanked Miriam for the tea and the conversation and rose to leave, Mel saying, "Don't get up, we'll let ourselves out, and we'll pop in the shop as we go and have a word with your father. By the way, has anybody thought to speak to your friend Judith? She might have spotted something more last night."

"Probably not," said Miriam, "the ambulance men didn't let her go with me to the hospital as she is not a relative, and she was too timid to insist – I'll write down her home address for you – she is a secretary at a main branch of the Westminster bank, so she wouldn't want visitors during working hours."

At the shop, they found Mr Schweitzer dealing with a customer, so they started to look at the display cabinets, where there was jewelry ranging in price and quality from simple paste clips to fairly elaborate necklaces and earrings. Mr Schweitzer was unlocking and locking the cabinets as he showed items to the customer, a rather well-to-do young person wearing a fur stole and a feathered cloche over an Eton crop, sitting on a chair by the counter and chatting constantly. Then she said, "Thank you very much, Mr Schweitzer, I will return when I have made my mind up. Good day to you!"

Chapter 30

The jeweller turned to Mel and Alex, saying, "Good morning, Madam and Sir, what can I show you today?"

Mel said, "I'm afraid we are not buying just now – maybe I will be able to cajole my husband into it later! We are a private detective agency, Crabbe and Crabbe, and we have just been upstairs talking to Miriam about the attack on her last night. We believe her assailant to be one of an organized gang of stand-over men, and we are working with the police to try and track them down."

"That's very good news!" said Mr Schweitzer, "Of course I will help in any way that I can! Did Miriam tell you that she believes that this was the same man who threatened us in this shop before?"

"Yes, she did, and his gold teeth will be very useful for tracking him down, but what would be better would be fingerprints – unfortunately he probably only touched your door, and there would be hundreds of confused prints on it already."

"But I may be able to help here," said Schweitzer, "you see this black velvet cloth that I have on my counter? It makes a good background when I'm showing jewels, so I keep it here most of the time. When this evil man was threatening me the other day, he lunged forward at me and steadied himself with both hands on the edge of the counter, pushing the cloth aside! When he left, I replaced the cloth, but I was too upset to think any more about it. It's possible that he may have left some prints, is it not? My only knowledge of fingerprints is derived from my reading of lurid detective novels when I have no customers!"

He lifted the cloth, to show that the counter top was polished mahogany.

Alex said, "Please put the cloth back carefully, Mr Schweitzer, and, if I may use your telephone, I will call my friend in the police and get a fingerprint specialist here straight away!"

Jimmy was very keen when he heard about this, and said that he would get someone there as soon as he could, "Meanwhile, make sure nobody else touches the counter – it might be a good idea to display the 'shop closed' sign until we've finished. See you soon – I'll come too, since I would like to speak to Mr

Schweitzer and his daughter some more – though I expect you have forestalled me on all of the pertinent questions! They want some advice on strengthening their security, I understand, too."

Once Jimmy and his expert had arrived, Mel and Alex excused themselves, Alex only pausing for a moment to ask whether there had been any results from examining the iron bar from the pawnbroker's.

"Yes, Alex," said Jimmy, "we did find something – I'll drop into your office later on and tell you all about it."

As Melpomene was feeling a little peckish, they decided to drop into Guiseppe's trattoria on the way back to the office, and enjoyed lasagne and a small carafe of house red.

They drew up at the agency at almost the same time as Jimmy Manley, and called for tea all round as they entered.

"Jam tarts, too?" Marjorie asked, and was slightly shocked when Mel said, "Not for me, thanks, but I'm sure Jimmy will partake!"

Winnie said, "As usual, there were several telephone calls, but one was from Detective-Inspector Manley, so you needn't answer it. Your Mama, Mel, was after her usual update bulletin – I told her you were out, and took the liberty of telling her of a few highlights, censoring the more exciting parts, like the murder. I hope I did right – I thought you would be better at reassuring her of your safety when you ring later. She said she was off to some sort of lunch in town with your Aunt, Lady Isabel and their other friend, the matron at the cottage hospital – I can never remember her name!"

"Anabelle Higgins," said Mel, "did she say what was the occasion?" "No, sorry – and I didn't think I should ask! There was also a call for Alex from a Mr Stanley, of Bloomfield's Dairy – I said you would ring back."

"Please get him for me, Winnie, it could be urgent!" said Alex, and when he answered had a fairly lengthy and earnest conversation with him. He eventually put the telephone down, saying, "That was very interesting news. Let's all sit down and grab our teacups and I will fill you all in."

"What Stanley said was that after my visit he decided to make more serious efforts at security, especially of the milk holding tanks, so he got two of his long-standing employees, a groom and a mechanic who looks after the pumps and conveyor belts, to make themselves comfortable for the night on a pile of sacks behind some boxes just inside the big doors leading to the railway siding, where they had a good view of the holding tanks. The mechanic had a big Stilson pipe wrench with him to use as a weapon if needed, but the groom said he would just rely on his fists."

"So did they catch anyone?" asked Mel.

"Yes in the small hours of this morning, an hour before the place was due to get going. The two guards had been taking turns to take naps, and the groom heard someone sliding open one of the big doors, so he woke up his mate, and they jumped on a guy as he pushed his way through the gap. They knocked him down and tied him up – and then found he was only a kid, maybe thirteen or fourteen. They telephoned the police and Stanley, and soon he was taken away for questioning, along with a tin of some liquid. They didn't know what it was, but it didn't smell like petrol or paraffin."

"This arrest must have happened since I left to go to the jeweller's shop!" said Jimmy, "Otherwise I would have heard about it – did Stanley say which station the police were from?"

"No," said Alex, "but the dairy is in Hackney – which would be the nearest nick to there?"

"That would be us, at Mile End Road! I'll telephone and ask a few questions – thanks Winnie – efficient as always! Oh Cec, Jimmy here. What's all this about an intruder at Bloomfields? – OK, keep him banged up tight till I get there. If he's only a kid, his parents should be informed – oh, all right, see you later."

Putting the telephone down, Jimmy said. "The silly kid won't say anything, not even his name – Cec Thomson says he's scared stiff and crying. I suppose the gang has put the fear of death into him if he blabs, poor kid. Cec has had the can of whatever sent by motorbike courier to the labs – it doesn't smell of anything, and nobody at the station was game to taste it – strange, that!"

"So, after all that excitement, what else can you tell us, Jimmy?" asked Melpomene.

"Only that iron bar we collected from Jacobson's pawn shop, Mel. It's human blood and hair all right, but until we find a body, we won't know whose."

90

Chapter 31

Melpomene had a further question for Jimmy Manley, "I can see, Jimmy, that that's about it for the milk side of the business, but what about Vanessa and Imogen's sabotaged Petri dishes? Did the fingerprint people come up with anything from the wreck of the lab equipment?"

"Yes, Mel," said Jimmy, "and even more than that! There were plenty of Imogen's and Vanessa's prints, and those of the lab attendants, but oddly enough, only on the autoclave and the incubators – none of those on any of the Petri dishes, neither the broken nor the intact ones! This seemed a bit strange to me!"

"Not to me!" said Mel, "I can tell you why, Jimmy. All of us who handled the dishes had clean cotton gloves on at all times! And there should have been some of mine on the apparatus, too!"

"Yours were probably some of the unidentified ones, Mel. We haven't got you on file at Criminal Records, yet – just watch it! As for the ones we took as checks, like Vanessa's, regulations say that they must be discarded after a certain time. If we kept everybody's, we could be accused of running a Police State!"

"You said you had more than fingerprints, Jimmy – what did you mean?"

"Aha! This is very interesting, Melpomene. On the bench among the broken glass, we found a grubby handkerchief with blood stains on it, that was twisted up as though it had been used to wrap up a cut hand. The lab people examined the stains and said it was human blood, type AB. This represents a very small proportion of the population of England, they told me, no more than 4 per cent altogether, while the most prevalent, type O, amounts to more like 44 per cent. So if we find a type AB villain, this would be useful evidence! The police and the law have only recently been paying attention to blood types – mostly, I must say, in cases of disputed parentage in connection with bequests and the like. But we should also remember that it was only in 1901 that the Fingerprint Branch was established at New Scotland Yard and look how important prints are now."

"But we have to catch someone first," said Alex, "before any of this can be used at all, surely?"

"You're forgetting that we keep a record of the prints of anyone who has been convicted of a crime – and they are all classified according to a set of well-defined characteristics, so that our experts can look at a new print and search through the records to find whether we have an identity for that person! The experts in the fingerprint department are doing such searches as we speak – I said that I would check with them later today – why don't I try now? Here's the number, Winnie, if you would oblige."

"Detective-Inspector Manley from Mile End Road, here, sergeant. Have your boys got anything on my prints yet? Right, let's start with the ones from the University College Microbiology lab – I guess you'll send me a written detailed report later, but have you turned anybody up from those yet? Good, good, let me write that down – do you have a current address for him? Last heard of late last year, eh? Well we know where he was recently! No more from the lab? By the way, do you folk keep blood types with the other records? Never mind – we shall not need it until we have him in the dock!"

Jimmy put his hand over the telephone mouthpiece and said, "We've got an old customer here, but he's only a small fish, I reckon. However he could lead us to more important gang members later. Now I'll see if they've had any luck with Mr Schweitzer's jewelry shop."

He finished his call and said, "We'll just have to be patient – they've got some good prints from the shop counter, plus some latent prints they want to intensify – they do this with chemicals, but it's all too technical for me. They say to call back tomorrow. Now I must get back to the nick – I want to see whether I can get anything out of this poor kid from Bloomfields dairy. Don't worry, Melpomene, I shall be gentle with him."

"Can I come too, then?" asked Mel, "As a special constable myself, I ought to know something about police interrogation techniques – and they must be related to social anthropology methods, after all!"

"Sure, be my guest, Mel – and a young kid like that might be less intimidated by a woman – we shall see."

At the Mile End Road police station, they went to the CID department to speak to Cec Thomson first. "We've put him in an interview room, rather than a cell, Jimmy – he was so terrified when he arrived that we thought that sitting him down there with a lemonade would quieten him. And WPC Sweet is sitting with him, too. You remember Jennifer, Mel, don't you?"

Cec took them to the interview room, where they found Jennifer Sweet, in plain clothes, sitting reading the paper, with the boy fast asleep at the table, head on arms. She said quietly, "I'm getting somewhere with him – he's told me his first name, anyway – it's Peter. If you stay, Mel, while Cec and Jimmy leave, I'll wake him up and see whether we two ladies can get his confidence now he's had a bit of rest – wakey, wakey, Peter, will you talk to us now?"

He sat up, opened his eyes and rubbed them with the back of his grubby hand, looking bewildered at the two women.

Mel said, "Hello, Peter, I'm Mel. It's Peter Williams, isn't it?"

"No, Miss, it's Peter Parsons – are you a teacher, Miss? I bin 'oppin' school lately, but it's not my fault!"

"That's all right, Peter. We're not after you for that – we know you've been doing things you didn't want for some men – don't worry, we won't let them do anything to you. Tell us about it and we can help you – the police are after them too."

The boy let out a great sigh and they could tell he was ready to open up. He let it all tumble out in a confused way, while Jennifer made short-hand notes and Mel prompted him whenever he paused.

After a while the flow slowed down, and Jennifer said, "Are you hungry, Peter? Would you like some milk and toast with jam on it?"

"Oh, yes please, Miss, I aint 'ad anythink since yes'dy, except a biscuit what the policeman give me when I came 'ere. Them men what took me to the dairy said they'd give me breakfast after, but o'course they never did!"

Jennifer said, "After that, Peter, we can get you taken home if you tell us where you live – will your Mum or Dad be there?"

"I ain't got no Dad, and me Mum does cleanin' mornins, so she won't be there yet – but she leaves the key tied to a string in the letter box."

"We want to talk to her, so we'll wait there until she gets home – is that all right, Peter?" He nodded, starting to cry again.

Chapter 32

They let Peter ride in front with Jennifer driving – he said that he had not been in a car very often before, except when the men took him to the dairy, and that was in a van. He guided her to a street in a run-down neighbourhood where they parked. He let himself into one of a row of houses, making sure that no one else could see that the key was hidden in the letterbox, and took them inside.

Melpomene was actually rather surprised, to her shame, that the house, although small and poorly furnished, was clean and tidy. Peter took them to the kitchen and proudly said, "If you want a cup of tea, I think me mum wouldn't mind if I made you one – I'm allowed to do it and we got a gas-ring. Mum does the cooking on the coke-stove, but it takes a while to light it and warm it up."

They both accepted, and were soon drinking tea from enamel mugs, sweetened with condensed milk. Peter asked them to sit down and apologized that he couldn't take them into the front room, because they kept it for best.

He said that his Mum usually got home later in the morning, unless she went shopping on the way home, and, indeed, after only about ten minutes, they heard her at the front door.

"We got ladies 'ere, Mum," he called out, so she was only slightly astonished to find Mel and Jennifer there. Jennifer drew her aside and explained that she was a policewoman, but that Peter was not going to get into trouble – they just wanted to ask him and Mrs Parsons a few questions, as they were mostly interested in tracking down the men who had taken advantage of Peter.

Peter made his Mum a mug of tea, and she told him to go and have a wash and then wait in his bedroom while she talked with the ladies.

"I wish I'd never let 'im go with those men!" she said, "They said they 'ad a job for 'im that'd pay ten bob – I thought it was just running errands, but they came for him late last night and told me they'd get 'im back in the morning and give him breakfast before 'e 'ad to go to school. I should've known then they was fishy – but they seemed straight up to me at the time."

94

"Did they tell you their names and where they were from, Mrs Parsons?" asked Jennifer.

"Yes, the main one said 'is name was Mr Challis, and 'is friend was Mr Clark, but o'course they might 'ave been making them names up. They never said where they was from, but they came in a van and I saw it had some Jerry name on the side, Katjammer or something like that."

"Could it have been Katzenberg's?" asked Mel. "Yes, that sounds right – all them Jerry names are a mile long! Last night they made Peter get in the back, where there was lots of boxes and tins – not like what you get from the grocers with peas and such, but big ones, packed in crates. Pete 'ad to sit on them. They said it weren't far to where they was going. Oh, I just remembered – I writ the number down as soon as I got back inside, 'cause I felt uneasy about it all! Let me see, I put it on the mantelpiece where I keeps the bills – here we are, you better take it, dear, since you're a policewoman!"

"Thank you, Mrs Parsons – that'll be a great help. Peter has already told us what happened when he got to Bloomfields' Dairy, but can you remember anything else about these men? How were they dressed?"

"Let me think now – Mr Challis 'ad on a nice suit and a collar and tie – with a tie-pin, too – rather flash 'e was. But his mate, Clark, had on ordin'ry overalls and workin' boots. It was 'im what was drivin' the van. Oh, and when they started orf, I 'eard Challis say, 'Go the long way round, Bertie, case there's anybody watchin' us!' – I thought this was fishy and all!"

"We'll say goodbye, now, Mrs Parsons," said Jennifer, "you've been very helpful. We'll say cheerio to Peter, too, as we go. Tell him he's got nothing to worry about, but we might want to speak to him again. Ah, here he is – goodbye Peter, you've done really well – do you know how to use a telephone box? Here's tuppence to make a call and I've given your Mum the ten bob that man promised you! And I'll write down the number of our police station. If you ever see either of those men again, try not to let them see you and give us a call. Ask for Mr Manley, or Mr Thomson, or Miss Sweet – that's me!"

Jennifer drove Mel back to Crabbe and Crabbe's and invited herself in for a cup of tea, saying, "I want to get the taste of condensed milk out of my mouth! If Alex is in, we'll tell him everything we found out from Peter and his Mum."

Alex was in, and over the tea and fruit-cake, Jennifer took out her short-hand pad and related Peter's tale, tidying it up a bit as she went.

"He said the men parked the van behind the dairy, by the railway siding. It was pretty dark by then, but there was some light coming through a window on the back wall, next to the sliding doors. They stood him on a box, and pointed out the big tanks – they must have been the milk holding tanks. They said that there was a lid on each one that was just clipped down, and that he would have no difficulty in getting one open. He was only to bother with one of the four tanks and leave the others alone. Then they gave him a tin, like a paraffin tin, he said, and told him he was to pour the whole lot into the tank. Then they left, saying that he should wait until they had gone, and then slide open one of the big gates, which were not locked."

"Of course, he was grabbed by Mr Stanley's guards before he could do anything!" said Alex, "The police took the tin for analysis – I wonder if they've come up with anything about the contents yet – I'll telephone Jimmy now and see whether he's heard from the lab!"

Jimmy answered straight away – he must have been expecting the call, and he was almost jubilant, "I just got some very interesting results on that tin at Bloomfields – not only what it contained, but where it came from! It's a good job none of our people actually dared to taste it – or they would be feeling very sorry for themselves!"

"Why, Jimmy – was it poison?" "Not really, Alex, it was phenolphthalein – do you know what that is?"

"I do!" said Melpomene, "we used to use it in the chemistry lab at school – it's an indicator that turns pink with acids! Why would they be putting that in the milk?"

"You're right, Mel!" said Jimmy, "but the lab people pointed out that it is also a powerful laxative – one mouthful and you'd be on the lavatory all night! But that's not all they told me. The tin had the remnants of a paper label on it, that the villains had tried to peel and scrape off – but on a scrap that was still attached, they could read part of a name – Katzenb... ! What do you reckon, Alex – does that remind you of anything?"

"Sorry to disappoint you, Jimmy – we already knew that!"

Chapter 33

"How did you know about Katzenberg's?" asked Jimmy Manley, "Did that kid tell you, or what?"

"Not quite," said Alex, "but as Jennifer was just telling us, his Mum spotted a sign on the van these blokes used to pick up Peter Parsons – that's the kid's name. She was also alert enough to take down the registration number – here it is, make a note, then you can have it looked up. Jennifer has full shorthand notes of everything Peter told us, so she'll fill you in as soon as she gets back to the station. I'll get on to Stanley at the dairy, and let him know everything – the guards he set would only know part of the story, up to the point where Peter was taken to the station. Jennifer told the kid he should ring you if he ever spots either of these characters again, but that's only a slim chance, I reckon."

Jimmy said, "So, Alex – are you going to follow any of this up with your contacts at Katzenberg's? You'd have to be very cautious – but I don't have to tell you that!"

"Yes, I was about to make a list of all the loose ends we need to pursue – I might have to check with you about some of them later, but meanwhile I'll sit with my social anthropology consultant and see what we can come up with between us. I'll talk to you later – you're still waiting for some fingerprint results from Schweitzer's, aren't you?"

"Yes, that's right – the lab's promised them for tomorrow. I'll let you know if they look helpful. I think that's about it as far as fingerprints go – but the lab said they'd pass the tin from Bloomfield's over to the fingerprint people now they've checked the contents. It's quite likely that whoever ripped the labels off has left them something in the way of prints."

Melpomene cut in at this point, "Tell Jimmy that I'd also like him to check an anonymous letter sent to me by way of my Mama, Alex – she forwarded it to the office yesterday and I'll give it to Jennifer now – it's somewhat cryptic as to content, but maybe if there are any prints on it this will tell us something. Mama says she's been very careful not to handle it too much."

Alex passed that on and rang off, saying, "I'm about ready for yet another cup of tea! How about you, Jennifer?"

"Better not, Alex, thanks very much. I'll get this letter handed over to Jimmy and see whether I've got any other jobs piling up at the station. There's a nice little case that Cec told me about, to do with shoplifting at a department store, which'll make a nice change – he was too embarrassed to take it himself, because it was in the lingerie department!"

Alex and Melpomene settled down round the table in the back office, and Mel took out one of her sheets of cartridge paper.

"Just lists from me!" said Alex, I don't think there's anything you could turn into a pretty chart. Let me see – I haven't had a talk with Gordon Salmon lately about his original query – though he's certainly had a lot of other business from us since then, what with autopsies and bullet-wounds and Miriam Schweitzer's equestrian adventures! How is your sampling going with Imogen and Vanessa?"

"At a halt, similarly, Alex – there's been all that business with the smashed Petri dishes, but unless Imogen has collected more swabs round the wards on her own, that side of things has been neglected. Actually, I would rather like to get out a bit – I was wondering about trying to track down Peter's abductors – we've got the number of the van and we know it's one of Katzenberg's, so if I were to hang around outside their yard, I might be able to spot the driver at least. You'd probably want to stay in character in your dealings with their management, so we had better work separately."

"In my view, Mel, just hanging round would be a waste of time, if you don't mind me saying so – and it would drive you out of your tiny mind hanging around with no guarantee you'd spot anyone. See what you think of this, as an alternative suggestion. You say you like masquerading as someone else – how about a turn as an inspector from the Factory Acts people?"

"Not keen, Alex – I should imagine that one would have to carry some sort of authorisation, and in any case, if a firm is sailing close to the wind, they would probably know all about the requirements and would soon see through me. But this suggestion has got me thinking, all the same – maybe I'll work on it and come up with something! I haven't appeared in public as a policewoman lately – I must ask Caroline to check my uniform over in case it needs ironing, but it's been hanging in the wardrobe since last time, so it should be all right. What reason would a policewoman have for visiting Katzenberg's?"

"Perhaps some responsible citizen reported seeing their van – whose number you have a note of – being driven without due care and attention on the evening when they picked up Peter – you needn't mention him, of course, but if the firm keeps proper records they should know who booked it out after hours that day."

"Terrific idea, Alex my love – I'll go home and get changed and then visit Katzenberg's – where is it, by the way!"

"It's in Hackney, not far from Bloomfield's Dairy, as a matter of fact, and fortunately it's an easy walk from the Hoxton tube station – its probably not a good idea for anyone to see you arriving in the Riley – we don't want it suffering the same fate as our good old Alvis! I'll write down the address and draw you a sketch map."

So, within the hour, Melpomene found Katzenberg's, which occupied a corner site, with a yard and garage up a side street, and presented herself to a man sitting at a counter inside the main entrance, engrossed in a copy of 'La Vie Parisienne' magazine. When she spoke, he looked up, and seeing it was not only a woman, but a policewoman, blushed and put the magazine away.

"How can I help you?" he said politely.

"Who is it in your firm who has charge of the vehicles and drivers? I would like to speak to someone at a responsible level."

"Well, Jack Blaikey is the garage foreman, but he just looks after maintenance and so on. What enquiries are you making, Miss – er – Constable?"

"I need to speak to whoever allocates drivers to vehicles, and authorizes their trips. I'm following up a complaint from a member of the public about an incident with one of your vans."

"In that case, Constable, I will ring up our Mr Houghton – if he can't help you, he'll be able to tell you who can."

He picked up a telephone and said "Henry, at the main entrance, Eileen – is Mr Houghton available to see a police lady? It's about a complaint."

Then, as, apparently, Houghton spoke to him, he said, "Right, Sir, I'll send her up." To Mel, he said, "Go through those doors and you'll see his office, first on the left."

Chapter 34

The glass panel on the office door he had directed her to bore the title 'Mr Claude Houghton, Assistant to the General Manager.'

Melpomene tapped on it and went in without waiting, to find a woman seated at a desk with a typewriter and document trays, who looked up, nodded toward an inner door and said, "Mr Houghton will see you in a moment, Constable, he has someone with him now." As she spoke, that door opened and a man, still turning his head and carrying on an irate conversation, presumably with Houghton, came out in a hurry.

He ignored Mel as he passed her, which was fortunate, because she couldn't help but stare at him – he had a pronounced stoop and a mouthful of gold teeth, which he was displaying in an angry grimace. She quickly recovered her composure and entered the inner office.

Houghton motioned her to take a seat and said, "What is this all about, Policewoman? Eileen said there was a complaint – I'm not sure I'm the right person, but please tell me and I'll see whether I can help."

Mel took out her notebook, saying, "I'm Constable Musgrave, from the Mile End Road station, Mr Houghton, and I'm following up a complaint from a woman who states that, two days ago, a driver of one of your vans abused her verbally when she had caught him talking to her young son, a boy of eleven years, and asked what he thought he was doing. She told our officer that the child was very frightened, and had told his mother that the driver had tried to force him into the van – she took the registration number, here it is – we had it checked, and it is indeed registered to Katzenberg's."

Houghton said, "Excuse me a moment," and buzzed his assistant on the intercom, "Eileen, please bring me the vehicle logs for the last two days."

She came in and gave him a folder, saying that the logs he wanted were the top two. He turned back a page and ran his finger down the columns, saying, "I see that that particular van was out twice two days ago, once in the morning to pick up some packages from the railway station, and once again in the afternoon, with no purpose entered, but with a note that the van was booked by a Mr Challis. The driver on that occasion was A. Clark, I see. Those names mean nothing to me – do you recognize either of them, Eileen?"

"No, sir, shall I ring Jack Blaikey at the garage? He knows all the drivers."

She went into the outer office, but after a very short conversation came back, saying, "Jack is puzzled – he didn't see the van leave the yard, neither of those names rings a bell, and that van was not returned to the garage until very late, after he had gone home! The night watchman told him that it was just left in the yard, with the keys still in the ignition, but that he didn't see the driver!"

Melpomene said, "Well, thank you both for trying, anyway – we shall just have to ask the complainant and her son if they can give us any more details. If you find out anything else, please let Detective-Inspector Manley at Mile End Road know – the number is in the book." She shook Houghton's hand and started to go, but as she was leaving his office turned and said, "By the way, Mr Houghton, I had the feeling that I have met your previous visitor before, but I couldn't quite remember his name – was it Wallace, or Willis, or something like that?"

"Nothing like that, Constable Musgrave – he's one of our reps – or used to be, actually, since I'm about to recommend to the general manager that he be sacked! His name is Phil Sterling. You might have run into him in a previous incarnation – he used to represent a catering supply company, so he could have sold tea and coffee and so on to your canteen at the station. He lost that job, I have just found out, for a similar reason that has caused me to seek his dismissal – he can't keep his hands out of the till!"

Melpomene thanked him and went into the outer office. She said to Eileen, "Another enquiry that has come to nothing, but through no fault of anyone here! By the way, as I told Mr Houghton, I think I recognized that Mr Stirling – do you happen to know his address, I would like to look him up!"

"I wouldn't advise it, miss! He's a nasty individual, if you ask me! But if you would really like to know, I'll ring my friend Ivy, she's in personnel. Just a moment, please."

She dialled a number and said, "Hello, Ivy, it's Eileen – no, it's not about afternoon tea – would you be able to tell a policewoman who I have here the address of that Phil Sterling – yes, I know he's a rotter! Oh thanks, Ivy, I'll see you later."

She wrote the address down on a slip of paper and handed it to Mel, saying, "Please watch your step, Constable, I wouldn't trust him any farther than I can throw him!"

As soon as she was back in the office, Melpomene told Alex she would tell him everything later, "I need to telephone Jimmy before I do anything else, even before I have a cup of tea!"

Jimmy Manley, as she expected, was very impressed with the information and said that he would get Sterling picked up straight away, if he was at home. "And if he's not there, we will just stake out the place and wait – we have enough on him to make it worthwhile putting quite a few men on the job. We know he's impulsive and probably armed, so I'm glad you resisted the temptation to go after him yourself, Mel! Once we've got him locked up, I'm sure Neville Butler and Miriam Schweitzer will have no trouble identifying him, so that's already a murder, an assault with a deadly weapon, and an attempted murder by horse trampling we can charge him with – yes I know the horse trampling thing is a bit steep – it'll probably just have to be another common assault. And that's before we start on all the demanding money with menaces charges!"

Alex, of course, was all agog to hear the full story, and very pleased that Mel hadn't had to let out anything that would queer his pitch at Katzenberg's. "Your contact Eileen could be valuable, too, Mel! It didn't need much wheedling on your part to get her talking, and she and her friend Ivy are probably a mine of information on everything going on behind the scenes at Katzenberg's. I shall keep my eyes and ears peeled when I go back and talk to Stephenson about taking up my role as an agent for his firm."

"What I'm wondering about now," said Mel, "is what the fingerprint boys will tell us about what they could find on the anonymous letter sent to my Mama, the phenolphthalein can from the dairy, and Mr Schweitzer's shop counter – but I'll take odds that the latter will come up with Sterling's prints again."

"To say nothing of what they'll find on the Petri dishes and the lab equipment!" said Alex.

102

Chapter 35

Before breakfast the next day, Jimmy Manley was on the telephone, in some triumph, saying, "Well, we picked up the bloke calling himself Phil Sterling! Of course, that's not his real name! He's on our books variously as Clive Watkinson, done for a number of shop thefts when he was in his twenties, and, more recently as Hugh Johnson, when he was foiled in an attempt to hold up an all-night petrol station. The attendant, who was counting his takings, objected to having a revolver pointed at him and threw a bag of pennies in Johnson's face, knocking out most of his front teeth!"

"Hence the gold fillings!" said Alex, "That's right!" replied Jimmy, "he was taken from stir to St Thomas's hospital under guard several times and the dental work was done courtesy of His Majesty's Prison Service! To return to my account, we went to the address you passed on to us, but of course he wasn't there. But a very obliging neighbour in his lodging house told my bloke that Mr Sterling was often to be found drinking in 'The White Hart' on Hackney High Street. To cut a long story short, I went there last evening with Cec Thomson. We spotted him in the public straight away – he'd obviously been trying to drown the memory of being sacked and was half seas over, so Cec grabbed him from behind and pinned his arms, and I was able to relieve him of his revolver."

"Congratulations!" said Alex, "Have you had the finger-print results back yet? I would be very surprised if the prints from Schweitzer's were not his."

"You're right, Alex, they are indeed – but we still haven't been able to match the ones from the phenolphthalein can, which were the same as some of those taken from the lab at University College. And they were able to lift some good prints from Lady Cynthia's anonymous letter, but no matches from Criminal Records yet – of course, the writer may never have been apprehended for anything."

"So what's next on your agenda, Jimmy?" asked Melpomene, who had been listening on the extension, "I'm thinking that I might get back in touch with Gordon Salmon – we've been rather neglecting his case recently, and we shouldn't forget that, after all, he is a paying client!"

"Good decision, Mel. What I'm doing next with your business – once I've cleared up my backlog of assorted house-breakings and car thefts, of course – is to see what can be discovered about the circumstances surrounding the supply of the wrong strength of Donnatal to Latham and Sons' pharmacy. The dispenser, Mr Stringer, has been cooperative, so we're going to track the Donnatal consignment back to the suppliers and see what might have been the mix-up. It could have been an honest example of carelessness – culpable all the same, given the outcome – or there might have been something sinister going on. Be assured, Mel and Alex, we shall make sure that we don't disclose any connection with you two, either in your real persons or in your various assumed characters!"

"Have you been told when the inquest will be reconvened?" asked Alex. "No, we shall just have to wait until we're summonsed. I hope that by then we'll have been able to ascertain more facts. Let's keep in touch – I'll certainly let you know when we come up with anything useful. I suppose you will be going to your office soon?"

"Yes, after breakfast – we haven't had a chance to start that yet. But Melpomene is going to telephone her Mama before we leave, to see whether she's had any more anonymous letters. See you later, Jimmy."

Lady Cynthia had to be called to the telephone by the maid who answered it, and sounded a little flustered.

"Oh I'm glad it was you who rang, Mel – I've been deliberately avoiding picking it up since what happened last evening, which I must say flummoxed me rather! A man's voice asked first whether he had the honour of speaking with Lady Cynthia Musgrave, and when I assented said something along these lines *'I have to tell you, my lady, that your daughter Melpommy is treading on dangerous ground! My associates are concerned enough that if she pursues her present line of enquiry, I fear that they will have no option but to eliminate her. As I said in my earlier letter, she is harassing the wrong people and would be better employed in going to the very top levels of the pharmaceutical industry. She is obviously unaware that she already has evidence in hand that could force confessions from key figures. I cannot say more, except to ask you to write down my next sentence accurately and convey it to your daughter without delay. Here it is – "It is not the managers, but the owners, who make the essential decisions for a company!" Have you taken that down, my lady? Please read it back to me, and that will be all!'* I did so, and he rang off immediately! Did you notice he made the same mistake with your name that he did in the unsigned letter before! As you can imagine, this has worried me stiff! I've spoken to nobody else, as I wanted to hear your reactions first!"

"Oh, Mama, I'm so sorry that our investigations have subjected you to all this anxiety! I shall certainly talk to our trusted advisors and try to work out what Alex and I should do next, but meanwhile, there are some things you should do here, Mama. Speak to Chief-Superintendent David Wilkinson and Stephen Buckmaster and tell them everything. Ask David if there is any way that your telephone calls can be monitored and traced. It may be too late to find the origin of the call last night, but it might be possible if the same caller tries again and the call can be intercepted. Will you do this? In any case, if you are like me, you will be happier doing things rather than just sitting and worrying! And if you get another such call, it might be worthwhile calling the exchange back right away and asking the operator if he or she can tell you where the call came from, even if it they can only tell you what exchange was concerned. I'll just have a word with Alex, who has been listening, and see whether he has any further suggestions – no, he's shaking his head. Please don't hesitate to call us again if there is anything else, Mama – we are going to the office now."

On the way to the office, Mel and Alex had a discussion and resolved that they should get back to Jimmy and ask him for further advice as soon as they got there. Mel went silent, pondering what else she should have said to her Mama.

The traffic was quite busy, and they came upon a hold-up where a car had run into the back of a milk-float, scattering broken bottles everywhere – fortunately nobody seemed to have been hurt, but the car driver was gazing ruefully at the damage to his radiator, which was emitting a plume of steam. The milkman was holding his horse's head, calming it down, and then led it and the float into a laneway, while several bystanders helped to push the car aside too, so that the traffic could start up again under the watchful eye of a policeman, who come up and took the particulars of both drivers, writing laboriously in his notebook with much licking of his indelible pencil.

"How exciting!" said Mel, "But it interrupted my chain of thought! I'm sure I was on to something!"

Chapter 36

As Melpomene and Alex walked into the agency, the secretaries, Marjorie and Winnie, seemed to be hard at work on various stacks of documents. Marjorie said "The new filing cabinets were delivered yesterday, so we're going through all the files and setting up new categories – we're making little labels to identify the drawers, and we also got in a whole carton of these new file folders that hang on runners, so we should be able to keep our work in much better order now. Winnie found stuff in the old cabinets with dates that went back to before Crabbe and Crabbe was even started – where they came from I couldn't say, so we've got one new drawer called 'Ancient History'!"

"This is excellent!" said Mel, "And now, here is a test for your system, you two – I've been thinking it's about time to go back and look at the papers that Gordon Salmon first brought us. We've done a certain amount of work on them, but my adventures with Vanessa and Imogen have set me off on a different track, and I would like to refresh my mind, so see what you can do over the next hour or so. Meanwhile, have there been any calls or correspondence we should know about?"

"Some bills, of course," said Winnie, "I'll put them on your desk, Alex – I have written the cheques for you to sign, so when you've done them I'll post them off. Apart from those, there is a very nice 'Thank You' note from Miriam Schweitzer, saying that she's walking much better now and is looking forward to seeing you at the trial of Mr Gold Teeth. Maybe you want to send her a hand-written note?"

"And a few telephone calls," added Marjorie, "One, only a few minutes ago, from Major Buckmaster, in Woodhampton, who wants to have a general chat, and also to talk to Mel about Lady Cynthia's anonymous telephone call. We've heard as well from Hugo Palance, who says he would like to have a word with Mel or Alex about a person who was intercepted at Dover with a trunk full of drugs – apparently Customs at Dover routinely inform their counterparts in Calais about such incidents. He said you could reach him at his office at the Sûreté – I checked, and we still have the number. Who do you want to speak to first?"

"Get me Stephen Buckmaster first, please," said Mel, "he may have some information about tracing telephone calls. Then we can both talk to Hugo."

"Nice to talk to you, Mel," said Stephen, "I had a long chat with your Mama just now, and I was able to assure her that there are ways of tracing calls. As a magistrate, I can authorise these attempts, and we can also call on the police if necessary. Fortunately, from this point of view anyway, the Woodhampton exchange is still manual – if it were automatic, like many of the exchanges in metropolitan centres nowadays, tracing would be harder. What we rely upon here is that all toll and trunk calls are logged and timed, so that the caller can be charged properly. Local calls are at a fixed rate, so that doesn't apply. So I've already spoken to the exchange supervisor and asked for a copy of the log for yesterday. They are going to send it to me by hand later this morning and we shall see what we shall see! How's the sleuthing business in general, Melpomene – any juicy cases?"

Mel brought him up to date on Miriam Schweitzer's adventures, without naming names, and on the subsequent apprehension of Phil Sterling, or whatever his name might be. She also mentioned the unfortunate demise of Mrs Pratt-Smithers, and their theories about the supply of her Donnatal – and this led into an account of the attempts to sabotage the dairy.

Stephen Buckmaster said, "I'm beginning to believe that you two have a magic attraction to interesting crimes – but I shouldn't feel envious, I suppose. As they say – be careful what you wish for! But you're losing your grip, Mel – you don't seem to have shot anybody recently – or are you just keeping it to yourselves?"

This badinage continued for a while, and then Stephen said that he ought to get back to work, but that he wouldn't forget about telling Mel what he could find out about the telephone calls.

Then it was Alex' turn, while Melpomene was greedily falling upon cups of tea and jam tarts, to ask Winnie to ring Hugo Palance at the Sûreté. He answered almost immediately, saying, "Bonjour, mon cher ami! How are you and the delectable Melpomene? It looks very much that we may be getting an opportunity to work together once more! I have recently been talking to Jimmy Manley, who amongst other matters tells me that you have been looking into some rather dubious suppliers of pharmaceutical products. So this reminded me of a case that your Customs people at Dover brought to the attention of our people in Calais. Maybe you have heard of it? A man was intercepted with a steamer trunk full of medications. He claimed at that time that he was working for a reputable English firm, but he was unable to produce an import licence or other supporting documents. I gather he is in custody awaiting proceedings."

"As it happens, Hugo," said Alex, "I have come across this case, but only indirectly. I was told by a former legal acquaintance that he has been retained to defend this man – but I don't know what stage the prosecution has reached. My interest in it is that it seems that the firm concerned is one of the pharmaceutical distributors that we are investigating from a completely different angle. I would dearly like to see us cooperating on this. Would you be able to come to London soon?"

"Certainement, Alex, I am happy to tell you that I am presently engaged with Scotland Yard in negotiations for England to join the International Criminal Police organization, which you might have heard was founded a year or two ago by several European countries, including France, Sweden and the Netherlands. Your friend, Jens-Olle Pedersen is representing Denmark in its efforts to join also. When the full body is formed, our little working group will be absorbed into it, of course, but until then, the Sûreté will continue to work with Jens-Olle and Adrian Fitz-Hugh of the Yard. This latest case, of the trunk-load of drugs, is right in our area of responsibility. I shall be in London in two days, and I will telephone you then, so please keep your diary clear! Might I now have a word with Melpomene?"

Mel she took the telephone, saying, "Hugo – how nice to hear from you! I caught the last part of your conversation and I hope I can be invited to the Yard, too! As well as the work with the pharmacy people, which we'll tell you all about face to face when we meet, we also seem to have crossed paths with the members of a Chicago-style stand-over gang, one of which our redoubtable Jimmy Manley has under lock and key, awaiting charges including murder, obtaining money with menaces and cruelty to horses! That last is a bit of an English joke, of course!"

"Thank you, Melpomene – I can hardly wait for the next two days to pass! Au revoir, ma chère Madame!"

Chapter 37

Melpomene and Alex started to go through the notes that Gordon Salmon had originally given them.

"You know, Alex," said Mel, "we have mainly been paying attention to problems with medicines – that is what led me to do the work with Imogen around the wards, and prompted you to start probing Katzenberg's and the other suppliers. What we have failed to follow up very much is his other category – suspected thefts from patients. These may not be related to the other problems, but they certainly rate as matters needing investigation, even if we – and Gordon – have been overlooking them recently. Let me see."

Mel started to rummage through the papers, which the secretaries had sorted into separate folders, and soon drew out a few.

"There's the lady I came across on my rounds with Imogen, who missed her romance novels, eau-de-cologne and lipstick, as well as that rather fat woman who claimed that her chocs and bickies had been swiped – that seems hardly a hanging offence, and she was better off without them, anyway, so perhaps the nurses removed them out of duty. Apart from those, though, we've got nearly two dozen reports of cash or valuables disappearing, mainly from bedside cabinets."

"Yes, Mel," said Alex, "there were some suspects named – the women who mop the floors, for example, though that may have been more a case of class prejudice than anything else – and wasn't there a question about the kid who goes round the wards selling papers?"

"That's right, but he is an easy mark, too – he's young, probably from a poor background, and so he's prone to being stigmatized. No, the ones who have the greatest opportunity to be light-fingered are the nurses and other ward staff, I'm afraid. I found, when I was going through the notes before, that Nightingale Ward had more than its fair share, and there were a couple of nurses' names that cropped up fairly often. Now is the time to follow up the duty rotas and do a thorough study of which names seem to correlate with these incidents – Gordon picked the rotas up from Matron some days ago and gave them to me."

Mel fetched herself another cup of tea and set to the task.

"While you're busy, Mel," said Alex, "I'll try Jimmy to see whether he has any more matches with those fingerprints – we already know about the ones from the Petri dishes and lab equipment – he says they match a known offender, but he thinks he is only small fry. What would be more interesting would be to find who handled the phenolphthalein tin."

"Not forgetting my Mama's anonymous letter, Alex!"

Jimmy was away from the station when Alex called him, but Cec Thomson answered and said that he was pretty sure that Jimmy had something interesting to tell about fingerprints and that he would ask him to ring them as soon as he got in.

"By the way, Alex," said Cec, "our Customs contact at Tilbury, Senior Preventive Officer Ben Fisher, was informed by his colleagues at Dover about their interception of the man with the trunk full of drugs. Ben thought we might like to know that his name is Donald McVitie, a native of Dumfries, known to the Scottish police, but only for traffic offences and the like – nothing criminal up to now. Apparently he is being held in a remand centre in Dover until charges can be brought."

"Thanks, Cec – give our regards to Jimmy and say we're waiting with bated breath for his news!"

Alex turned to Mel, saying, "The mention of Dumfries rings a bell – I wonder if this McVitie was working for Dalgleish and McDonald, the firm that Mr Latham mentioned, who he thought were in the process of trying to take over Hathaway and Woodruffs as well as Katzenberg's? This makes me think that I should talk to Monty and see what else he's willing to tell me. He was a bit cagey last time the subject came up, but that was in a social setting. And it also reminds me that I was about to approach Hathaway's again, now we know a bit more. David Woodruff was pretty affable with me over drinks earlier, so he might be inclined to open up about the takeover and Dalgleish and McDonald. I'll give him a call in the morning and arrange to see him after I've been back to see Mr Stephenson at Katzenberg's. He never raised the question of a takeover when I was there before – all he said was that Katzenberg's were under pressure from their parent company in Luxembourg. I suppose that all this stuff is hush-hush because they have to protect their standing on the stock exchange!"

"Are you going to telephone Monty Petherick this afternoon?" asked Mel, "Perhaps he'll be in court – or could you try his chambers – did he tell you which Inn he belonged to? If not, how would you find this out?"

"I know the Clerk of Chambers at Gray's Inn," said Alex, "I doubt that Monty has his chambers there – it is rather too reputable a place for him! But the Clerk might be able to look him up, or give me a lead – it's worth a telephone call."

But before he could do that, the telephone rang with a call from Jimmy Manley, apparently in an optimistic mood, who told Alex, "Success on two fronts with the prints, Alex! There were some good prints on that tin – and we soon found whose they were, a habitual crim called Paul Andrew Timmins, who is prone to housebreaking, and – get this – shared a cell in Pentonville for three or four months with Phil Sterling, alias Clive Watkinson, alias Hugh Johnson, the man with the expensive mouth! What's more, we discovered where he's living now, so a couple of uniforms went to pick him up for questioning. And Cec Thomson and Jennifer Sweet are on their way in a car to see whether they can persuade Mrs Parsons and her son Peter to come to the nick and identify him!"

"Well done, Jimmy! You said success on two fronts, what was the other?"

"Put Mel on, Alex, it mainly concerns her. Right, it's about your Mama's anonymous letter, Melpomene. It took the fingerprint boys a while to develop some latent prints from that letter, but they managed, with the use of some chemicals, to get a good left thumb and index finger of a size typical of a female – it looks as though she was steadying the paper as she wrote. And these were enough to make a match with enough common features to make a solid identification. Do you want to have a guess? I'll bet you a tenner you won't get it!"

"Oh, Jimmy – stop it, do! I've got no real idea, but since you're being so mysterious, I'll make a reasoned attempt! It's someone who's fairly educated, judging by the language, even though she has apparently no familiarity with Greek mythology. She knows about our investigation, that it has to do with the pharmaceutical industry, and that we have been talking to hospital people. A further point is that her prints are on file, so there must be a reason for that, too! I guess Matron Stevenson, assuming she has a Home Office licence for controlled drugs!"

Chapter 38

Detective-Inspector Jimmy Manley laughed out loud at this, "Bravo, Melpomene – an excellent try, but although it came close, it didn't hit the target! Why would Matron Stevenson be communicating with Lady Cynthia – and how do you explain the fact that the follow-up telephone call was in a man's voice! Do you want another go, or shall I put you out of your misery?"

Melpomene was never one to refuse a challenge, so she said, "Leave it with me for another little while, Jimmy, and I'll ponder some more. I'll go and scribble a bit, so I'll pass the telephone back to Alex."

Jimmy said to Alex, "I won't spoil things for Mel by letting on yet, but I've got some other things to talk about while she exercises 'ze liddle grey cells' as your colleague Hercule Poirot would put it. The first item is that we are driving to Dover, Cec and I, to talk to Donald McVitie, the man with the trunk. Do you think you, and possibly Mel, would like to come with us?"

"Just try and keep us away!" said Alex, "When will you go?"

"Tomorrow would be best, I think, because the day after that I have an appointment to meet with Adrian Fitz-Hugh's specialist group at Scotland Yard – apparently Hugo Palance and Jens-Olle Pedersen will be there too. You and Mel will be going, I suppose?"

Just then, Melpomene threw down the scraps of paper that she had been fiddling with and exclaimed, "I've got it – let me talk to Jimmy again!"

Back on the telephone she said, "I claim the ten-pound reward – I know the perpetrators now! Alex won't be pleased, because I think he has taken a shine to her, but I'm now convinced that Elspeth McCracken is one of them, in cahoots with Henry Jackson, who – just because of his appearance – we've been calling the 'rural dean'! We need to make further enquiries, but I think that those two are trying to divert our attention away from the hospital, because they have been running a profitable little – or maybe not so little – racket defrauding the drug suppliers! How they got onto my Mama, I don't know just yet, but I shall find that out in good time!"

"Congratulations, Mel!" exclaimed Jimmy, "You guessed right about the Home Office licence, too – that's what put us on to her. I had to get special permission to peruse those records, but luckily our friend Howard Anderson in the Foreign Office was able to pull a string or two with his opposite number in the Home Office, so we found Elspeth's entry easily – their lists are a lot shorter than the criminal records ones, naturally. While we were about it, I had a search made for Henry Jackson, but his nose is clean – so far! He was probably the one who made the telephone call to Lady Isobel – all we know for sure is that Elspeth McCracken wrote the letter."

Alex had a point to make, taking the telephone briefly, "This certainly looks like a reasonable hypothesis so far, but what we really need now is some hard evidence! We need to get access to the orders and invoices and get them audited by someone who knows what to do, and the trouble is, we can't ask either McCracken or Jackson for these without tipping them off."

"Once we've sorted that out," said Mel, "I've thought of a suitable independent accountant we can call on – Philip Seaward, who audited the books of the St Luke Embassy after all the trouble we discovered there. He's obviously *au fait* with what I believe is called in the trade 'forensic accounting' – or, in lay terms, unearthing swindles. And I suppose he will able to get authority from the police to examine bank accounts, unless they have set them up under false names."

"Even if they have," said Jimmy, "a good accountant would know how to follow the trail of transactions leading from one account to another. Let's leave that worry to Mr Seaward! Will one of you contact him and put him in the picture, please? But don't actually engage him until we've got some more to go on."

After Jimmy had rung off, Mel said, "Guess what, Alex, I'm famished after all that thinking! Where shall we lunch – Guiseppe's as usual, or do we want to break new ground?"

"Let me try and run down Monty Petherick's chambers first, Mel, then we may be able to kill two birds with the same stone. Winnie, have you got the number for Gray's Inn? I'd like to speak to the Clerk of Chambers, please."

That gentleman was very obliging, recognising Alex from his previous visit, but was able to confirm that Monty was not a member there. "You could check at the Law Courts, sir. If he is by any chance appearing today, they will have him on their running sheet. I'll tell you the best number to try, if you would like to note it down."

The clerk at the Law Courts checked, but apologized that couldn't find the name Petherick on that day's list.

"Ah, well," said Alex, "I'll try him at home this evening. Meanwhile, lunch calls! Are you fixed for lunch, Marjorie and Winnie?" Marjorie's Mum had packed a lunch for her as usual, and Winnie had bought a slice of veal-and-ham pie and a jar of Picalilli on her way to work, so Alex and Mel headed off for their favourite trattoria.

When, an hour later, they got back to the office, Winnie was hopping up and down over an urgent telephone call. "Would you ring your Mama as soon as you can, please Mel? She sounded rather excited – but not upset, I think."

When Melpomene spoke to her, Lady Isobel was indeed in a happy mood, "I had another telephone call from Mr X, that I took in my office – but I had made an arrangement that if I gave a certain hand signal to Mavis, my secretary, she would use another telephone to ring our switchboard, who would be all ready to put the machinery in motion for tracing the call. We had set this all up after Stephen Buckmaster told us what would be involved!"

"That sounds wonderful, Mama! Did it work?"

"It certainly did, my pet! The call was traced to the business office of, guess what? Finchley General Hospital! They didn't have a name to give us, but I recognised the voice, who merely repeated his earlier warning, in much the same terms – that we should forget about bothering about the hospital but go after the owners of the supply companies! But, strangely, he pronounced your name properly this time – not Melpommy, but Melpomene!"

"Curiouser and curiouser!" said Mel, "What could possibly have put him onto me? As far as the hospital knows, I'm Henrietta Musgrave, and Alex is Alan Robertson! All I can think of is that somehow they have found out about Crabbe and Crabbe. Keep watching this space, Mama – I shall certainly let you know as soon as we find out anything. Meanwhile, are you all right? You really sound fairly cheerful. If you carry on with this line of good work, we'll soon be able to add you to our letterhead as an honorary consultant!"

Chapter 39

Soon after Melpomene and Alex got to the office the next morning, Jimmy and company arrived in a police limousine for the trip to Dover. Cec travelled in the front seat next to the driver, and Jimmy took one of the jump seats in the back, so he could talk easily to Mel and Alex.

"Have you found out any more about Mr McVitie?" asked Mel.

"Not so much about him, but some more about the trunk and its contents," replied Jimmy, "the lab boys found that what he was carrying were bulk cartons of opiate tablets, for example, morphine and codeine, plus some barbiturates, including your favourite Donnatal. But unusually, he was also carrying a large tin of raw opium, which could only have been destined for smoking by unfortunate addicts in opium dens, such as those in Limehouse in the East End of London."

"How about identifying labels on the cartons or the tin?" Alex wondered, "Tracking down the suppliers might help us to find the intended destinations. Presumably McVitie had acquired the goods in France, unless he brought them from somewhere further east by train, which is quite possible. Were there any stickers on the trunk, Jimmy?"

"We'll have a chance to look when we get to the remand centre, Alex – all his possessions, including his personal effects and clothes have been put into bond. The cartons and the tin of opium went to the lab while the testing was being carried out, but they would have come back to the bond store as soon as the testing was complete, this has probably happened already. They were all dusted for fingerprints before they went to the lab, they tell me. We shall have a chat with my opposite number at the Dover station, Detective-Inspector Weldon, before we go to see McVitie. I've spoken to him on the telephone, and it sounds as though he knows what he's about."

They drew up in the forecourt of Dover Central police station just in time to forestall Melpomene from dying of hunger, so she was very glad to hear Inspector Weldon suggest that they talk over morning tea in the canteen. Once they had all been provided with mugs of tea – from a pot, not an urn – and scones with Devonshire cream and strawberry jam, Vernon

Weldon opened by saying that McVitie was a puzzle to him in more than one way.

"You must judge for yourselves, but I must admit that this man is very different from the usual smugglers that we see. The Customs and Excise people are very smart at picking suspicious travellers out, and many of them are handed over to us as soon as C and E have conducted initial interviews, and in some cases, body searches. Most contraband arrives in luggage, of course, but items of high value or often concealed about the person – or, begging your pardon, Madam – actually in the person!"

"Don't worry about my susceptibilities, Inspector," said Melpomene, "I can guess what you're talking about! How, though, does Mr McVitie differ from your usual customers?"

"This is very subtle, you should understand. When you have been dealing with crims of various kinds for as long as I have, you can see them being sheepish, or shifty, or defiant, or in some other way behaving differently from your average person. This bloke was so matter-of-act that it almost amounted to boredom, and even when he was confronted with the discovery of the contents of the trunk he behaved as though he was simply conducting a legitimate activity, saying that he was bringing the goods in quite openly for a respectable importer – but he stopped short of naming that company. When we asked to see the relevant documentation, like an import licence, he looked puzzled rather than guilty before admitting he didn't have any."

"So that was the point at which he was turned over to you?" said Alex.

"Yes, I had already been called in – we try to have men at the docks whenever a ship of any size docks – watching out for other illegal matters, not only smuggling. For example, we arrested a married couple from Spain travelling on a false passport the other day, and we spotted a guy only this morning who we recognised from a photograph that had been circulated to all forces – he has been wanted for robbery with violence for over six months and was still carrying a cosh. He'd been on holidays in Nice and Monte Carlo for a while, but had spent all his money at the tables and was coming back for more."

"Why was he coming back to England? Couldn't he have carried on his trade over there?" asked Mel.

"We asked him that, but he said that he was much more afraid of the police in France – he'd been spun all sorts of yarns about mates who had finished up on Devil's Island! So, if you're ready, let's go and see Mr McVitie. I have arranged for him to be brought to an interview room here, so we don't have to go to the remand centre. Follow me, please."

Melpomene said, "We make rather a crowd, all of us. What if Cec Thomson and I go and have a look at the trunk and his clothes and other possessions – I assume they're here at the station – while Jimmy and Alex join Inspector Weldon in interviewing him – what do you think?"

"Excellent!", said Weldon, "And afterwards it'll probably be time for lunch – on me – at a nice little place I frequent that's close by, and you and Jimmy can tell me what exciting things are going on in the Big Smoke!"

The trunk, the cartons of medicines, the tin of opium and various belongings were in a locked store-room, presided over by a uniformed sergeant, who pointed out that everything but the drugs had been gone through thoroughly and put back into the trunk carefully. "You can spread it all out on the table here," he told Mel and Cec, "every item, including the trunk itself, has been checked for fingerprints, so you don't need to wear gloves or take particular care in handling anything."

The steamer trunk was the sort that opens up when stood on end, with a space for drawers on one side, now empty, with the drawers missing, and a hanging space for clothes on the other, now with just one suit and a shirt. Mel started by taking out the suit and going through all the pockets, finding two silk ties, one in a military stripe, the other plain blue, a pack of playing cards, a pouch of pipe tobacco and a box of Swan Vestas. "No pipe?" she wondered quietly. There was also a pair of gents' black brogue shoes, well polished.

She asked the sergeant, "Where were the cartons of medicines, and the tin of opium – below the suit and in the drawer space, I suppose?"

"That's right, Madam, the shoes and some underclothes in that laundry bag were on top of the cartons. And the cartons and tin were wedged in with crumpled-up newspapers."

"I do hope you kept the newspapers, Sergeant!"

"Yes, they're on the table, tied with string, and labelled 'Keep'!"

Chapter 40

While Melpomene and Cecil Thomson were looking at the trunk, Alex, Jimmy and a civilian shorthand writer, Edwina Morton, were taken by Inspector Weldon to an interview room, where they found Donald McVitie, a short, stocky man with frizzy ginger hair, wearing grey overalls and sitting at a table reading The Times – somewhat to Alex' surprise. The warder, who had opened the door when Weldon knocked, said briskly, "On your feet, McVitie, you have some visitors with questions!" To Inspector Weldon he said, "I'll just sit in the corner in case you need me, sir."

Weldon said, "You know me, Mr McVitie – this is Detective Inspector Manley of the Met, and Mr Crabbe, a private investigator – both are interested in hearing your explanations. Miss Morton is here to take notes – beginning, please Edwina, with a record that this interview commenced at 11.45, today's date."

Jimmy took the man through a re-telling of the circumstances at the immigration counter of the dock office. McVitie nodded at each point, occasionally adding a comment. He spoke with a pronounced Scottish accent, probably Glaswegian, thought Alex. When the story reached the point where the trunk was first opened, Alex asked, "Did you have to use a key to open the trunk, Mr McVitie, or was it already unlocked?"

McVitie looked a little startled and said, "You canna go leaving your luggage unlocked on a ship, sir, if you dinna want it to be rifled! I had the key, and I used it, o' course."

Alex continued, "So you are sure that the contents were untouched since you packed the trunk – where did you do that, by the way – at your hotel in Calais, or where? And how did you receive the cartons of medicines, were they brought to where you were staying, or did you have to pick them up from a dépôt?"

"I wasna staying at Calais, sir, I came to the docks by train, wi' the trunk and another valise."

"All the way from Luxembourg was that?"

"No sir, changin' at Paris – but I never said I came from Luxembourg, did I? Why for did you think that, sir?"

"I thought that, simply because, according to the list of your personal effects we've been given, you had a label on your valise that read, 'Chemins de Fer Luxembourgeois' – but maybe that was from a previous trip? So, did you or didn't you come from Luxembourg this time?"

"Yes, sir, so I did. The company that engaged me is there, but I was told that there were questions of commercial confidence, so I shouldn't disclose their name. I ken now that I was foolish tae agree to this, because look whaur it's landed me!"

Jimmy Manley spoke up, "Maybe it's not too late for you to redeem yourself, Donald – tell us everything and we might be able to charge you with a lesser offence leading to a shorter sentence! So what company was it that put you up to this, and who were you supposed to deliver the goods to?"

McVitie seemed to relax at this, "Could I possibly have a cup of tea?" he said, "And forby I can tell you the whole story, as much of it as I ken."

As the warder left, saying "Cups of tea all round, is it?" Melpomene and Cec appeared at the door, Mel saying, "And us, too, please!"

Then she and Cec were introduced by Inspector Weldon and took their places at the table. Mel said, "I would like to ask you something else, while we're waiting. Mr McVitie, do you smoke a pipe?" He shook his head. "So the tobacco pouch and the matches were merely meant as distractions, right?" He nodded, looking abashed.

"I thought as much, so I carefully took apart the matchbox, and what I found, scribbled on the underside of the tray, was what looks like a telephone number – here. Can you tell us about this, Mr McVitie?"

"That's my contact in London – I don't know his name, I just have to mention the word 'Dumfries' and he'll recognize me."

"There's another thing," said Melpomene, "to do with the pack of cards you were also carrying. When I glanced at it, I thought it looked like a new pack, but then the cards felt a little too tight as I pulled them out, so I counted them and found that there were fifty-five all told. A standard pack, as we all know, has fifty-two, plus two jokers, so I looked carefully through and sorted them into suits and – lo and behold! – there was an extra Jack of Clubs! What can you tell us about this, Mr McVitie?"

119

"Y'are verra sharp, Miss! Hold that card up agin the light, please – can you see any pin-pricks?"

Mel did as he said, squinted at it and said, "Can't see any, Mr McVitie!"

"So you must have the wrong Jack of Clubs – try the other one."

Melpomene did so and then exclaimed, "Yes, I see them! Just under the 'J' in two of the corners. What is this all about?"

"I ken well that's there's no hiding anything from you, Miss, so I'll tell you all that makes sense to me – and that'll leave some gaps, nae doot!"

Cec walked over and murmured in her ear, "I've been talking to Jimmy, and I'm now going to slip out and try that telephone number – but I'll be very careful how I answer – I might not even say a word, we'll see!"

He left the room, and Melpomene continued, "That's very wise of you, Mr McVitie – what would help us the most would be the names of companies and people. We have our suspicions, so if we can strengthen them or confirm them completely that will save us a lot of time. I'm sure that the police will take this into consideration when charges are brought – I can't promise that you will get off Scot-free – oh, I suppose that expression could be a bit insulting to your country – please don't take offence!"

"I won't, Miss, there's many worse things been said tae me! If I tell you where I picked up the goods, and where I was going tae take them if I hadn't been pounced upon, how would that be? Well, In Luxembourg there's a gey big warehouse – I was given the address and told to ask for Monsieur Dupont – I dinna think that was his true name – and I was to show him the Jack of Clubs as a sign. Well, that I did, and he gave me the whole steamer trunk, already packed, and he called and paid for a taxi to take me to the train station, too. He said I would find a suit and other stuff in the trunk, and I was to put the cards and anything else I wanted to keep hidden in the pockets of the suit and the toes of the shoes. "

"Oh!" said Mel, "I missed them!"

"Nae matter, Miss, I only put some French banknotes there – not much of an amount. And I was to take all this to a company called Hathaway and Woodruff, at an address in London."

Chapter 41

Alex had been quiet for a while, but now he spoke up, "There's still a couple of missing links here, Mr McVitie! Who was it sent you off on this expedition in the first place? Who gave you the address to go to in Luxembourg and supplied you with the playing-card to use as proof of your identity? And when you've told us this, if you do, I will probably still be confused about their motives!"

"I'll tell you the whole story, Sir. It was like this – I have a friend who is the office manager for a big Dumfries company called Dalgleish and McDonald. One evening, as we were enjoying a dram together in a bar, he asked me whether I was free for a job that might take a few days. He knew I had recently lost my position as a rep at a knitwear firm, when it was taken over by a bigger company, so I was gey keen to have a crack, and not too bothered at what! I told him 'aye' and he said I was to come to the head office at nine o'clock the next morning and he would introduce me to a Mr Hamilton."

"Did your friend tell you what it was all about?"

"No, sir, he did not – mebbe he didna ken hisself. Anyway, I turned up as arranged, and was shown into Mr Hamilton's office. He asked if I had been abroad before and did I have a passport, which I had, because I used to take knitwear samples to big department stores in Holland and Belgium. Then he explained what he wanted me to do, but he never said why – and I didna think it was my place to ask. He said he would give me the tickets to get all the way to Luxembourg, and enough money to travel from there to Calais, cross the Channel and get to London."

"Was that all he told you?" asked Melpomene.

"No, miss, he said it was all very confidential, because there were business rivals involved – but he assured me it wasna illegal. Then he gave me the address I was to go tae, and how I was to show the Jack of Clubs to a Monsieur Dupont, who would give me further instructions. As I've already told you, this all happened and went smoothly, right up to the time that I was stopped at Dover."

Said Alex, "So you really never found what was the purpose of this exercise? You knew that Dalgleish and McDonald are wholesalers and distributors of medical supplies – did you never wonder why they chose to send you, instead of going through their usual agents and procedures? They must be importing items from the Continent all the time through legitimate channels and with the proper import documents, so why was this different?"

"I'm sorry, sir, but I canna say! Nobody telt me a thing!"

After that, the general opinion was that there was no more to be gained from further questioning, so McVitie was escorted out of the room for a trip back to the remand centre. As he left, Detective-Inspector Weldon said, "You've been very cooperative, Mr McVitie – you will get news about charges and court appearance just as soon as decisions can be made by my superiors, and your barrister will also be informed."

By this time, Weldon decided it was lunchtime, so they all got into Jimmy's car and the driver was directed to a restaurant near the harbour. They took a table that had been booked for them, in a position where they could talk without other patrons overhearing.

As soon as they were settled with glasses of one sort or another, and had chosen from the menu, Melpomene said, "Now, Cec, I've been wondering how you got on with that telephone call. What was the outcome?"

"Well, it was very interesting! I asked the switchboard lass at the station here to get the number, which she did with no delay. A woman answered, saying, 'Hathaway and Woodruff, Mr Moody's office,' so I just said, 'Dumfries'. The woman said, 'Oh yes – Mr Moody is at lunch, can I have your number so he can call back?' so I said 'Not to worry, I'll call again'. Then she said, 'I'll give you his home number – I know he is anxious to hear from you', and she told me a number, which I put in my notebook."

"Well done, Cec!" said Mel and Jimmy simultaneously, Jimmy going on to say, "It looks as though our idea that this might all be bound up with possible take-overs by Dalgleish and Co. might be along the right lines – but we still don't know the reason for the unconventional method of transport. Any ideas?"

"I do have a somewhat wild idea!" said Melpomene, "But it might just be that – wild! What if this is some sort of a ruse to denigrate Hathaway and Woodruffs or even some of the others, so that their shares will go down in value, or even to drive them into bankruptcy, so that Dalgleish and McDonald can pick them up at a bargain price, along with their customer lists, their purchasing and shipping departments and so on. Is that just my fantasy or what?"

"So our Mr McVitie is just the bait in a trap?" said Jimmy, "Or a sacrificial goat, depending on your point of view. And what they are aiming at is to create a scandal involving illegal importing of controlled drugs by Woodruffs – or downright illegal drugs, in the case of the opium."

Melpomene nodded, "And they'll leak this all to the gutter press so that it will be blown up – I can see the headlines now – 'LOCAL FIRM IN OPIUM DEN SCANDAL' and so on! I'm thinking that, if Jimmy and Mr Weldon and Scotland Yard play their cards right – sorry about the pun, it just slipped out – then it might be possible to thwart this plot and start to track down the perpetrators. I'm starting to think that there must be some individuals within one or other of these companies who are hoping to make big money somehow!"

The waiter started to bring their meals, so Vernon Weldon said "No more shop – let's enjoy our meal and speak of other things. Are there any golf players among you – oh, only you, Alex, perhaps we should resist boasting about our prowess and find a more general topic!"

The time passed very pleasantly until Jimmy said, "We ought to be heading back to London soon. Thank you very much for today, Vernon – we learnt a great deal from Donald McVitie. Tomorrow Alex, Melpomene and I have a meeting at the Yard with a group interested in drug trafficking that includes some police officers from France and Denmark, so we shall certainly share this case with them and see whether it will lead us further. We'll keep you posted, of course, as much as we're permitted."

Hands were shaken all round, Melpomene even bestowing kisses on Jimmy and Cec, who wriggled a little bit at the experience, and the car was soon headed back North.

Mel and Alex were dropped at the agency and went in to answer a stream of questions from Marjorie and Winnie.

Chapter 42

Of course, what the secretaries wanted to know was everything about the trip to Dover, but Melpomene refused to say a word until she and Alex had been given cups of tea. Winnie disappeared to make the tea, and Marjorie said, "While we're waiting, there've been a couple of telephone calls that seemed important, one from Deputy Commissioner Fitz-Hugh at Scotland Yard, and the other from Mr Petherick – he gave us the number of his chambers, where he'll be until about four o'clock, and his home number in the evening."

"Thanks, Marjorie," said Mel, "please get me Adrian Fitz-Hugh first – if a snooty secretary answers that it's *Sir* Adrian's office, tell her that it's the *Honourable* Melpomene Crabbe calling."

When Adrian answered, he said, "Oh good, Melpomene, I'm glad you got back in time to ring me. I wanted to tell you we've set up a meeting tomorrow morning, and if you're agreeable I'll send the car for you at about nine-thirty. Hugo Palance and Jens-Olle Pedersen will be there, and I know they're keen to hear about the steamer trunk incident at Dover – I take it that you were able to extract some useful information from this McVitie? I look forward to seeing you and Alex tomorrow."

Alex received this news from Mel happily and said, "Now Marjorie, Monty Petherick, please – try his chambers first, even though he's the kind of chap who's inclined to slope off early, if I'm any judge!"

Petherick answered straight away, so Alex said, "Hello, Monty, finally we get to talk – we've been chasing each other back and forth over the telephone for ages, it seems! You tell me what you want to say, and then I'll give you an account of our meeting with your client Donald McVitie this morning."

"First of all, Alex, I'm no longer going to represent McVitie – his solicitor, Reggie Withers, got in touch with me a day or two ago and called me off, without giving me any real reason, just saying that circumstances had changed. I had to accept this, there was nothing I could do. A pity, because I had done a certain amount of investigation on his behalf – I shall certainly invoice him through his solicitor for out-of-pocket expenses, even though there is little chance of being paid! There was one thing I wanted to pass on to you, Alex, but I'll leave this until you've told me your story – you may already have come across it! So tell me your opinion of Mr McVitie, and what you found out, if you're at liberty to share it with me."

"To sum it up in a phrase, Monty, Donald McVitie is being used as a dupe! Whoever employed him had no need of someone to bring those medicines from place to place, whether or not they are controlled substances, because there are legal ways of doing that, which are being used every day by pharmaceutical companies! I believe that it was the tin of raw opium that was the whole point, and that everything else was put in as a distraction!"

"What brings you to this conclusion, Alex?"

"I've been looking this up, Monty, and have found that opium was decreed to be illegal by the 1919 International Opium Convention of The Hague, incorporated in the Treaty of Versailles and now endorsed by the League of Nations. And the Dangerous Drugs Act of 1920 brings Britain into line with its obligations under that Convention. In short, raw opium is an absolutely forbidden substance! Now what was it you were going to tell me, Monty?"

"Like you, Alex, I have been doing some digging, and found that opiates and barbiturates like those McVitie had in the trunk are routinely shipped between countries all the time, along with properly assigned import and export licences issued by the governments concerned. His only offence with regard to these stemmed from his not being in possession of such licences, and I was going to argue in court that he was not obliged to carry such licences with him, and that, if any offence of that nature was being committed, it was by Dalgleish and McDonald, who employed him as their agent. But the opium is a different matter – it's out and out illegal – nevertheless I was still prepared to argue in court that McVitie was tricked into carrying it – but then his solicitor, Mr Withers, said that his client had decided that his case was hopeless and that he would not contest it. I was a bit doubtful about this, so I telephoned the remand centre, introduced myself and asked when it was that Mr Withers had seen McVitie since our first visit. They consulted their records and said that, as far as they knew, the only visitors he had received recently were from the police, when they arranged for him to be interviewed at Dover police station – this morning, presumably. So I'm inclined to believe that Reggie Withers has been got at by someone."

"Very interesting! Perhaps Mr Withers needs to answer a few questions – have you tried to contact him, Monty?"

"Of course! But his office claims that he is away somewhere, 'talking to important clients', and said they would inform him on his return, but didn't know when that would be. I have my doubts about that, too!"

"One more question, Monty. How was this Reggie Withers approached by Donald McVitie? Would the police have advised him to retain a solicitor?"

"You had better ask them, Alex – I have no idea – all I know is that Withers approached me to act for him in any forthcoming court case. Together we went to speak to McVitie at the remand centre, but we got very little from him, other than a plain recital of how he was recruited, how he picked up the trunk in Luxembourg and how he was picked up by the Customs people."

"Yes, we got this story, too. He seems so naïve that I find it quite likely that he just allowed these arrangements to be made, without taking any active part in them. Thanks, Monty – I'll get back to you if I need anything else. Before you ring off, tell me Reggie Withers' address and telephone number, please – I take it you would have no objection to us trying to contact him?"

Alex said to Mel, who had been following this conversation on the extension, "Curiouser and curiouser! Winnie, can you get Detective-Inspector Weldon at Dover for me?"

Weldon confirmed what Alex had suspected, that Mr Withers had simply arrived with Mr Petherick at the police station, and had been directed to the remand centre, claiming that they were representing Donald McVitie, but without providing any letters or other corroboration of this. As Vernon Weldon said, "We had no reason to think otherwise!"

Melpomene thought a bit and then said, "This poor fellow is being set up every step of the way – somebody is plotting all this behind the scenes! My guess is that this is all part of a conspiracy – most likely, as I said before, to discredit Hathaway and Woodruffs so that their assets can be picked up at a bargain-basement price! It will be very interesting to hear what Adrian Fitz-Hugh, Hugo and Jens-Olle say about this when we meet them tomorrow morning!"

"You're right, Mel! My head's buzzing already. Let's go home!"

Chapter 43

But they were not going to get away as easily as that – as they opened the office door to leave, the telephone rang again, and Winnie picked it up, answering, "You've just caught them, Doctor Salmon – do you want to speak to Alex or Melpomene?"

"Either or both, thanks, Winnie – it's fairly serious!"

Alex took the telephone, and Mel picked up the extension earpiece. "Go ahead, Gordon!" said Alex, "What's all this about?"

"The police have just visited the hospital and arrested Elspeth McCracken! They also asked to see Henry Jackson, but his secretary told them he was out on business, she didn't know where. I had the impression that they wanted to grab him, too. Elspeth's assistant was told to contact Detective-Inspector Manley at Mile End Road if she wanted more information. I then tried Jimmy's number myself, but someone at the station said that he was tied up for the rest of the day. So I thought you two might have a passing interest in all this!"

"You were right, Gordon – but did the police say nothing further?"

"No, but I can't help feeling a little guilty, because I realised it was I who let slip to Elspeth that it was the Crabbe and Crabbe agency who were investigating my concerns about irregularities on the wards. I didn't let on, however, who Henrietta Musgrave and Alan Robertson really were!"

"Thanks for that, Gordon – please don't belabour yourself about your slip! We'll get onto Jimmy as soon as we get home – we have his home number, and he won't mind! When we know more, of course we'll fill you in."

Once they had hung up. Melpomene said, "As soon as we get home, I'll telephone Mama and put her mind at rest – I'm pretty sure now that she will not receive any further anonymous telephone calls or letters!"

When they got to the flat, Melpomene surprised Caroline by declining a cup of tea, saying, "After I've spoken to Jimmy Manley!" Fortunately, Jimmy was at home, and had plenty to tell.

127

"No doubt Gordon has told you we nabbed Elspeth McCracken," he said, "but since then there have been further developments. We cleared the staff from all the management offices and sent them home and then we sealed the doors and filing cabinets and left one of our men on guard. In the morning, we'll get in touch with Philip Seaward and commission him to do a thorough audit of the hospital books – I've no doubt that he will find some leakages of funds into bank accounts held by Jackson or McCracken."

"So, what about dear Henry Jackson?" asked Melpomene, "I gather he was not in his office?"

"We asked his secretary where he might be, but either she didn't know or was being loyal, simply saying he was out on a business call. I had one of my detectives pay a visit to his home, but got a similar story from his wife, so my man thanked her politely and left and then found a spot from where he could watch the place, after calling in and letting us know. If Jackson tries to telephone Elspeth, her secretary has instructions not to let on that she's been nabbed. And if he rings his office, there's nobody there to answer. He's using his hospital car, which he's entitled to do for business, so we've got a call out for that, too. One way or another he'll turn up, and then we've got him! We'll be holding both McCracken and him in the first instance on charges of extortion, in terms of *'writing libellous letters or letters that tend to provoke a breach of the peace'*. No doubt there will be plenty of other charges to come! You'll have to excuse me now, Mel, I'm getting furious looks from Mavis who wants me to come to the table before my dinner gets completely cold! Shall I see you at the Yard in the morning?"

"Certainly, Jimmy – I'm glad you're coming! Enjoy your dinner!" she said as she hung up.

"Now, I have two more calls to make – tea, please, Caroline!"

Mel first reassured her Mama, who was obviously relieved, and then brought Gordon up to date, who told her that in the unlikely event of Jackson turning up at the hospital he would take appropriate action.

That business done, Melpomene and Alex enjoyed a meal of what Mrs Mountain referred to as "Boil yer base", which was delicious, as always. They then listened to a Mozart concert on the wireless, but were a little disappointed that there was nothing of interest to the agency on the BBC News that night!

As they were ushered into the special meeting room at Scotland Yard the next morning, they were greeted by Adrian Fitz-Hugh, Jens-Olle Pedersen and Hugo Palance and introduced to an upright bearded gentleman called Karl-Heinz Friedrichs, who explained he was representing the Grand Duchy of Luxembourg in the ongoing negotiations to set up an international police service, but was also particularly interested in a couple of pharmaceutical establishments that had recently been set up in Luxembourg by foreign firms.

"I'm slightly ashamed to reveal that certain companies, not only in that industry, are endeavouring to take unfair advantage of my country's commercial laws, which tend to be rather more lax than those elsewhere. I should say that there are serious efforts in train to rectify this situation, but the wheels of government and the law tend to turn rather slowly!"

After welcoming refreshments, the first hour or two of the meeting, dealing with the formation of international collaborative mechanisms, though quite interesting, were not what Melpomene and Alex were looking for. Nevertheless, they paid attention and even, in Alex' case, took notes. Adrian Fitz-Hugh apologised for not providing detailed documents, explaining that complete confidentiality was paramount at these early stages.

And then, morning tea and coffee were called for – saving Melpomene's life, as she muttered, but with a smile on her face – and giving an opportunity for the exchange of items of gossip.

They were about to settle down around the table to embark on the next items on the agenda, when a secretary, with a tense expression on her face, came in and spoke to Adrian, who then said, "There's an urgent call for you, Jimmy – please take it in the next office!"

Jimmy did so, and within a very few minutes was back, saying, "I'm afraid I shall have to rush off, ladies and gentlemen – there has been a startling development – an attempt at arson at Finchley Hospital! To further disrupt this meeting, I am going to propose that Melpomene and Alex accompany me to the scene, as it has direct consequences for one of their current investigations. Again my apologies – will you come with me, Mel and Alex?"

They were already on their feet as Adrian said, "Yes, go! – We'll reconvene later – our guests will be staying here for a while!"

Chapter 44

As the police car approached the hospital they could see policemen blocking off the street, and two fire engines, one with crew members busy putting its extension ladder up to windows on the first floor. At least two of the windows at that level were broken, with black smoke gushing out. The other engine was reeling out fire-hoses with firemen dragging them into the main entrance of the building.

When the driver drew up, Jimmy got out of the car and approached a fire officer who seemed to be in charge, and Melpomene and Alex saw them have a brief conversation. Then Jimmy came back and said, "We've been cleared to go inside, as long as we don't get in the way. The flames are mainly out by now, I'm told, but one of the wards close by is being cleared of patients because of the smoke. The target of the attack was the business office next to the stairs. My guess is that this was an attempt to destroy all the financial records – you might surmise who instigated this and to what purpose! When all the excitement and running about is over, we may be able to put together some sort of account of events."

There was not much to see in the ground floor foyer area, just the hoses being run up the stairs, and three or four people sitting on a bench being attended to by nurses, among them a fireman breathing with the aid of an oxygen mask and a policemen having his hands bandaged up.

Jimmy knew him, so went over and said, "Hello, Osborne, are you fit to talk – did you see what happened at all?"

"Yes, Inspector, I was actually the one guarding those offices. I was sitting reading the paper when I heard the sound of breaking glass from inside. Then I could see through the glass panels in the door that flames had started up inside the office, so I pushed the fire alarm button and unlocked the door. This was not a good move! As soon as I started to push the door open there were flames licking up it. I managed to shut it, but I had been burnt a bit. Then the firemen started arriving, and they had protective clothing and gloves, so they were able to open the door and start hosing down. I left them to it, and someone brought me down here and put something on the burns and wrapped up my hands, as you see. I think some other people have been taken to Accident and Emergency – do you know where that is?"

"Oh, yes!" put in Melpomene, "We are regular visitors there!"

As they made their way to A and E, they had to step aside to make way for a trolley bearing a figure draped from head to foot in gauze. One of the porters pushing it said breathlessly, "We got to get this poor bloke to the ambulance quick – he's off to the burns unit at UCH, and it's touch and go whether he makes it!"

Gordon Salmon spotted them as they came in, "Well, I think we're coping with most of the immediate cases – mostly superficial burns, with just one or two old dears who've inhaled smoke who we've put on oxygen just in case. Did you see that trolley on its way to the burns unit?"

"We certainly did!" said Alex, "What happened to cause that man to be so severely burnt?"

"Come into my office, and be prepared to take notes, Jimmy – I think he was one of the villains responsible for this outrage – but he may already be paying the price for his sins. While I and my staff have been anointing burnt people with various unguents and bandaging them up, I've been putting together some sort of a picture of what happened. The police and fire brigade arson specialists will come up with something more professional, of course, but this is what I have gathered was the course of events. Cups of tea? I could do with one! Thanks, Patricia, that's kind of you."

"We already heard a little from Constable Osborne, who was guarding the offices," said Jimmy, "but please tell us more."

"I'm pretty certain that it was all started with a number of beer-bottles full of petrol being lobbed into the offices, smashing the windows on the way. The first few were just thrown as they were, but then the crooks started to light petrol-soaked rags wrapped round the necks of the next lot, and throw them in to start the fire in earnest. Unfortunately for one of them, his aim was bad, and the flaming bottle hit the window-frame and fell back on him, soaking him from head to foot with burning petrol. The two firemen who dragged him in here tried to put him out, but sustained burns to their own hands while doing so. They told me the whole story as I tended to them, after I'd done what I could for the victim!"

They finished their cups of tea and thanked Gordon, who returned to attending to burns and a couple of minor accidents caused by people running about in panic in the smoke-filled gloom.

Outside, they found a uniformed police inspector talking to the senior fire officer who had taken charge of the brigade work. Jimmy introduced himself and asked whether any of the perpetrators had been detained, apart from the badly-burned one.

"Afraid not!" said Inspector Coogan, "They all slipped away in the confusion – my men were keeping would-be spectators away, and my friend, Fireman First Class Withers here, also had his hands full, as you might understand. But we've just been saying that we both noticed a green van parked at the end of the street, which took off as soon as the fire-engines arrived. I didn't think of taking its number, I'm afraid."

Then a girl of about thirteen or fourteen, who had been hanging about watching all the commotion, heard what he said and called out, "If you want to know about that van, I took the number! I noticed it special, because it's the same as me Dad's greengrocer's van, a Morris Commercial One-Ton – we only got it this year to replace the old army Leyland we had before! I can tell you its number, and I also noticed the name of the company painted on the side – it was Hathaway's, like Ann Hathaway's Cottage that they told us about at school when I was younger!"

"You're interested in motors are you?" asked Melpomene, "What's your name – what you've told us could be very important!"

"I'm Cissie O'Malley, Miss, and me dad is teaching me to drive – only in the yard o' course, I shan't be old enough to get a licence for a year or so yet. Me Aunty Ethel was an ambulance driver in the War – you should hear some of her stories!"

"Can you tell the number and anything else you noticed to my husband here – he'll write it down in his notebook. Your address too, in case we want to speak to you again."

The girl was obviously feeling quite important, and told Alex everything, including the address of her Dad's shop! Melpomene kissed her, and Alex slipped her a shilling!

They agreed to telephone Adrian Fitz-Hugh about reconvening the meeting, then Jimmy's driver ran them back to the office.

Chapter 45

Of course, the first order of business was to relate the whole story to a fascinated pair of secretaries, over more tea and jam tarts. At the end of the account, Melpomene said, "I'm puzzled that Hathaway's displayed their van so openly – even without our observant little girl, they must have known there was a risk that their name would be spotted!"

"That assumes that it was someone from that firm who set up the whole thing!" said Alex, "What if it was instead part of the plot to destroy Hathaways' reputation? You remember that Donald McVitie gave us the number of his contact – it led to someone called Moody, who wasn't there when Cec rang – so I'm wondering whether he's somebody working undercover to ruin the company. I'll try ringing that number again!"

He looked it up in his invaluable little black book, and, as when Cec Thomson had tried, a woman answered. When he said "Dumfries" she transferred him to a man who said "Moody here – I thought you were locked up, McVitie!"

"No, no!" answered Alex, in an attempt at a Glasgow accent, "I'm let out on bail, you ken! I just heard on the wireless that there's been a muckle great fire at Finchley hospital – that was no your work, was it, Mr Moody?"

"How would you know about that, McVitie? I was told you were supposed to be just a messenger, not part of the plot!"

"Weel, Mr Moody, when you're the big mon runnin' a show, it's best not to let the little folk ken too much! Mysel' I didna ken aboot yoursel until someone mentioned your name tae me, and that were only yesterday. Are you sayin' it wasna you that had the fire set?"

"I'm saying nothing at all – you can think what you want, for all the good it will do you! Goodbye, McVitie – and watch your back!"

Alex hung up and told the others briefly what had transpired, Then he said, "Maybe Jimmy can try David Woodruff, and see whether he knows about the van – if I were to ring him he might smell a rat!"

"I think I have a better idea!" said Melpomene. "What if WPC Henrietta Musgrave were simply to turn up at Hathaways' front office, playing it straight, saying that a van with the company name on it was seen near the hospital fire, and could anyone tell her whether the crew saw anything that might be helpful in the police enquiries."

"I'd go for that one!" said Winnie, "People tend to get serious when they are questioned by the police. Was there really an item about the fire on the wireless news?"

"Not as far as I know!" said Alex, "I just made that up! How did my accent sound?"

"A bit like Will Fyffe on the BBC," said Melpomene, "but not bad for a few moments – I doubt whether you could keep it up for very long! There's another thing we must attend to first, though – the auditing of the hospital books, if there are any left! I'll telephone Philip Seaward and see whether he can do it."

He said that, of course he was willing to have a try, as forensic accounting was his speciality, and when Mel pointed out that there had been an intense fire, he explained that, contrary to what one might think, paper, especially thick stacks of it in metal filing cabinets, did not burn easily. "I'd be more concerned about water damage, actually. As soon as the police and fire authorities release the offices, I'll come with my assistant and make an assessment of our likely success. Who will be paying, Mel? Not your agency I hope – I can be rather expensive!"

"I'll check, Philip, but I'm sure that the hospital trustees would be anxious to have their affairs cleared up – they've probably been suffering losses over some years without being aware of it. When I find out, and discover when you will be allowed in, I'll let you know – thanks for being so willing to help."

Mel rang off and said, "Now let's see when we're expected at the Yard again – I'm sure Adrian, Hugo and Jens-Olle will be entranced by all this! Can you try Adrian Fitz-Hugh's number, for me please, Marjorie?"

Fitz-Hugh indeed sounded very interested, "But we're all going to the canteen for lunch now, Melpomene – I should point out that the one here is a cut above the usual police-station canteen – what if I send the car for you at about two-thirty, would that leave enough time for you to have your own lunch?"

"That'd be fine, Adrian – we have a favourite trattoria not far from this office – see you all later! Should we contact Jimmy Manley, or is he already coming?"

"He's already with us, Mel, and he has some news that will interest you two particularly – I'm looking forward to hearing it myself!"

Mel and Alex were among the first people to arrive in the conference room, and while they were waiting for all the others, the gentleman from Luxembourg, Karl-Heinz Friedrichs, came over to them and said, "A lot of things seem to be clicking into place now – before lunch I received a telephone call from the high director of the Luxembourg Ministry of Trade to say that he has ordered the financial records of two large pharmaceutical concerns there to be sealed and investigated, one of them being Beestler Holdings, the parent company of a Scottish firm you may have come across – Dalgleish and McDonald! I'm awaiting more details, which are being brought to me by official courier."

Once they were all seated, Adrian Fitz-Hugh called the meeting to order and said, "It looks as though this group is now moving into a phase of information exchange and pooling – we have to consolidate before we can do anything further about setting up collaborative mechanisms. I will first ask Detective-Inspector Manley to bring us all up to date about the evidence that has emerged from this morning's dreadful arson attempt – Jimmy?"

"Thanks, Adrian. I'm glad to be able to tell you that there have been very few serious injuries resulting from the fire, with the notable exception of one of the instigators, who is at present in intensive care with burns to over half his body. The surgeons at University College Hospital burns unit, who are always conservative with their judgments, estimate that he has less than a forty per cent chance of survival. We will not be able to identify him until the doctors permit his forensic examination. Turning to other matters, we have made some progress over the strange case of the green van. We wondered how it was that such an obvious clue was presented to us, but, partially owing to the sharp eyes of a Miss Cissy O'Malley, we have discovered that the van was taken without authority from Hathaways' motor pool and abandoned some streets away from the hospital. In my humble opinion it was a deliberate distraction, intended to draw attention away from the real perpetrators of this serious crime."

Chapter 46

"Thank you, Jimmy," said Adrian Fitz-Hugh, "I believe that Hugo Palance wants to tell us about some recent developments on his side of the Channel – Hugo?"

"You will all know," said Hugo, "that we at the Sûreté take pride in our methods of surveillance, and I'm happy to tell you that we have had a recent success. After we missed picking up M. McVitie, I established a watching brief on the express train service from Luxembourg to Paris, paying special attention to unaccompanied passengers headed for the cross-channel ports with items of luggage that seemed excessive in size for one person, while our colleagues under Herr Friedrichs are making their enquiries into the Luxembourg firms. At this time of year there is not a great tourist traffic, and we specifically avoided scrutinizing family groups. We had one or two false alarms, but yesterday my men spotted another single traveller with a large steamer trunk. The customs agents were alerted before he set off for Calais, and when he arrived there they discovered that he was carrying a number of cartons of medical products – but on this occasion he was able to produce a seemingly valid licence. The agents, nevertheless, made an exhaustive search and found that, as well as the items listed on the manifest, the trunk also contained an unmarked carton of a crystalline substance. To cut a long story short, this was found, on analysis, to be cocaine – another banned drug, like opium. But the real sting in the tail is that the whole consignment was addressed to Messrs Hathaway and Woodruff and marked 'For the Attention of Mr Bruce Moody' – they have apparently abandoned the 'Dumfries' code-word approach!"

"What about the passenger with the trunk?" asked Melpomene, "Was he detained and identified?"

"Detained, yes – but not identified when I spoke to my men last – he said his name was Samuel Smith! They will let me know, of course. He was not a Scot this time, but spoke with a regional English accent that my agents did not recognize."

Jimmy said, "That's enough reason for me to make a telephone call and get Mr Moody arrested and questioned about that matter and the fire – if he can be found – we are still looking for the Reverend Jackson, but haven't been able to catch him yet. Excuse me!" and he left the room.

"What's this about the Reverend Jackson?" asked Adrian.

"Oh, just a private joke!" explained Alex, "He is really Henry Jackson, the finance manager at Finchley Hospital, but Mel and I think he looks like a rural dean! He and Elspeth McCracken, the hospital pharmacist, will be charged with issuing threats to Melpomene's mother, Lady Cynthia Musgrave. It appears that, as well as milking hospital funds over the years, they are at the heart of the conspiracy that's emerging to discredit and devalue Hathaway and Woodruffs, so that Beestler Holdings, through Dalgleish and McDonalds, can pick up the firm for a song."

"And we all thought that the pharmaceuticals industry was as ethical as its products!" said Jens-Olle Pedersen, "I suppose that, having found that the textiles business, the art market and the diplomatic community can all harbour evil at their hearts, we shouldn't be at all surprised! I even wondered, when the name of the Reverend Jackson came up just now, whether I was going to have my faith in organised religion tested!"

Jimmy Manley came back into the room and made some announcements, "First, a couple of successes! Our surveillance of Henry Jackson's house has paid off – he was caught climbing into his place over the back fence – our lads are not as easily fooled as that! So he will be charged along with Elspeth McCracken, in the first place with issuing threats, and then with various counts of embezzlement and fraud, depending on what evidence can be recovered from the scene of the fire. Then the mysterious Mr Moody has been picked up from Hathaway's and will be interrogated about the fire, as well as by someone from our major frauds division, who are also going to approach the head office of Dalgleish and McDonalds in Dumfries. Lastly, some news for you, Alex and Melpomene – the inquest on Mrs Pratt-Smithers is to be reconvened at the High Barnet Coroner's Court in two days – you will get an official summons, of course. Is there any more tea on offer?"

After these bombshells, the rest of the discussions were not as interesting, but Mel and Alex stayed to hear that the establishment of the International Criminal Police organization was now almost certain to go ahead under the aegis of the League of Nations, as soon as the participating governments could ratify the various protocols and agreements. When they were dropped back home it was close to dinner time and they sat down to enjoy a meal that Mrs Mountain simply referred to as, "baked ham with honey glazin' and cloves".

After dinner, Alex went through some of the notes in his book, saying. "I ought to try and fit in another meeting with Mr Stephenson at Katzenberg's before the ripples from Hathaway's about Moody's arrest reach him and cause him to clam up! I want to see what I can find out about the dealings with their parent company in Luxembourg that he spoke of – I assume he was referring to Beestler Holdings."

"Be very careful, Alex! These shady businessmen are possibly all talking to each other in a panic now, after the recent events – and they are capable of reacting viciously to protect their interests! There are other things that would be good to clear up before we go to the inquest, too, so we can get them off our minds."

"Yes, Mel – I'd like to be there when Philip Seaward has his first look at the burnt-out offices at Finchley Hospital, hopefully tomorrow some time. With any luck he'll be able to judge how comprehensive his examination of the files might be. Apart from the fire and water damage, the important entries will have been disguised to avoid immediate detection – but that's the sort of thing that experienced forensic accountants should be able to untangle. We shall see!"

"I'm going to try ringing the Burns Unit at UCH, too, Mel. It would be good to know whether that arsonist is going to pull through or not. I made a point of getting the number last time I was talking to Gordon Salmon, and he said I could mention his name when I enquire."

But after reaching the Unit and having a brief conversation, Alex put the telephone down and said, "That's one villain who won't have to face justice – fate has already caught up with him – he passed away early this afternoon, still unidentified – but with his fingerprints taken, although the person I spoke to said that his hands were badly burnt, so she wasn't sure whether the police experts were able to get much of a result. I expect we'll be told in the fullness of time."

"Not a pleasant way to go!" said Melpomene, "But I suppose he deserved everything he got – at least we can be thankful that the fire had no other victims, neither innocent nor guilty."

138

Chapter 47

As soon as Melpomene and Alex had reached the office the next morning, the doorbell rang and in came Jimmy Manley, who said, "I tried ringing you at home, but you had already left, so I came straight here. I've got a search warrant for Elspeth McCracken's house – she lives on her own – so I thought you might like to come with me and see what you can turn up."

"We certainly would, Jimmy!" said Mel, "Did you have anything in mind particularly, or is it just a fishing expedition?"

"Well, I'm hoping there will be letters or other documents to do with her dubious activities, but also I know that Gordon Salmon had been collecting all sorts of notes about unexplained events around the wards, so there might be some physical evidence to discover. Let's go and find out!"

Elspeth's house was an unremarkable bungalow in a quiet street, with a pocket-handkerchief-sized patch of lawn and a few weedy border plants in the front yard. Jimmy unlocked the front door, telling one of the uniformed policemen he had brought with him, PC Browning, to mind the front, while the other, PC Arnott, went round the back to make sure they would not be disturbed from that direction.

On the mat just inside the door there were several letters, which Jimmy carefully put into a large envelope, picking them up by the corners so as to touch them as little as possible. "We can go through these later at our leisure – they may not tell us much, but I would hate to miss some message from other members of the gang, if there is one."

There was a sitting-room with a settee, easy chairs and a roll-top bureau, two bedrooms, one almost empty except for several cardboard cartons, and a large kitchen-dining room, as well as a bathroom and lavatory.

"Should we split up to save time?" asked Melpomene, "Bags I the bedroom, and Alex can go through the desk, which leaves those cartons and the kitchen for Jimmy. How about that? If any of us finds anything interesting, we can discuss it together. We've all got something to write on, I suppose – I brought a note-pad."

"Sounds good!" said Jimmy, "There's a little key here on Elspeth's key-ring , see if it fits the bureau, Alex."

Everything became quiet for an hour or two, until Mel emerged from the bedroom and announced, "I've found several items that might be useful evidence, and a veritable treasure-trove in the wardrobe! I'll go and make us cups of tea, and I'll tell you about my discoveries in the kitchen."

"Good thinking!" said Jimmy, "I'll tell my men outside that they can have tea as well, on the condition that one of them pops to the corner shop and gets some milk!"

"Ask them to look out for jam tarts or something, too!" said Mel, "I had a poke about in the kitchen and there's not much to eat, apart from an opened packet of Peek Frean's Bourbon Creams, which are probably stale by now."

Melpomene put the kettle on, and by the time it had boiled, PC Browning was back with the milk, a fruit-cake and some mince tarts. He and his mate decided to take their tea and snacks and eat them in a sunny spot in the back garden. Jimmy and Alex settled down with theirs around the kitchen table and turned expectantly to Mel, Alex saying, "You go first, Mel – it sounds as though you had some success!"

"First," said Mel, holding up a cloth laundry bag, "there are these!" and she poured out on the table a collection of small objects, including purses, powder compacts, lipsticks, and cigarette lighters. "At a guess, these have been pinched from patients' bedside lockers at Finchley – what do you reckon? And just to strengthen that hypothesis, there are these!"

She lifted a carton onto the table, tipped it up and produced a stream of books, saying, "Agatha Christie, Ethel M. Dell, Georgette Heyer, Josephine Tey, and some authors even I have never come across – perhaps Alex would recognize them! Some of them are library books – I suppose the borrowers had to pay fines on them as well as recovering from their hospital stays!"

Alex laughed, saying, "We'll be able to settle a lot of Gordon Salmon's pilfering cases now! But those are evidence of rather minor sins – what I found in the bureau drawers seemed much more serious. I've sorted them into piles in the sitting room, but I can tell you that one category is what looks like duplicate invoices for rather large shipments of medical supplies, for instance 'Sixty gross of morphine ampoules', with a price that made my jaw drop – we shall need qualified people, like Gordon Salmon or Vanessa Spring to tell us their significance, and we shall have to search the hospital files for corresponding receipts and delivery dockets, if our accountant friend can sort them out. What concerns me is the simple fact that McCracken had seen fit to take these documents home with her."

Jimmy spoke up at this point, "I shall have to arrange for an expert forensic medical team to come in and completely comb through the place – what I found in the spare bedroom were cartons full of a jumbled mixture of bottles and packets of many different sorts of medications, including the famous Donnatal of the prescribed strength, which, as I remember, was ¾-grain tablets. I think we've done sufficient work here for one day, ladies and gentlemen! I'll leave one of my men to guard the place until it can be properly searched."

He went to the back door and called, "I'm going to leave one of you in charge – you two blokes had better toss up who stays first – I'll arrange for a relief as soon as I get back to the station. Let's check that the telephone's still working here before we go."

"Good idea!" said Melpomene, "I'll take the opportunity to check in at the office and see if anything interesting has happened while we've been here. Hello Winnie – how are things going there? Any dramas?"

"Not really, Mel, the postman just came with the usual letters and bills, and apart from those, there's a heavy brown-paper parcel addressed to 'Melpommy Musgrave', that was brought by a courier on a motorbike."

"Don't open it, Winnie, whatever you do! Put it down carefully somewhere in a corner and stay well away! I'll tell Jimmy and he will probably know the right people to contact. On second thoughts, you two should get out of the office and wait for us in the street! Don't let anybody else go into the building! We shall be there in fifteen minutes or so!"

She told Jimmy all about it, and after he had made a telephone call, they all bundled into the police car and set off. Jimmy said to the driver, "The station first, Lenny, we'll pick up Sergeant Simmonds – he worked in bomb disposal during the War – and then back to Crabbe and Crabbe. You can break the speed limit if you want, I'll cover you!"

Chapter 48

When the police car pulled up at the Agency, there were Winnie and Marjorie sitting at the bottom of the stairs looking very anxious. Jimmy said, "This is Sergeant Mal Simmonds, ladies, give him the keys and tell him exactly where you have left the parcel."

Mal nodded as they explained and then said, "I'm going to leave the doors open, in case I need to make a quick getaway. Now, before I go up, tell me a couple more things – is the parcel wrapped in brown paper in the usual way, with string? You said it was brought by a motorcycle courier – did he handle it gingerly, or just give it into your hands like any parcel? Did you have to sign for it, and, if so, do you remember the name of the firm?"

Marjorie said it was just like any other parcel, but quite heavy, that the courier was carrying the parcel in a knapsack and didn't treat it particularly carefully, that they weren't asked to sign for it, and that he had no badge or name-tag or anything to identify who he was working for.

"But I did notice that he was quite young and spoke with an educated accent – I wondered if he was a student picking up a bit of extra money, but I didn't ask him!"

Sergeant Simmonds went up the stairs carrying a case like a doctor's bag and disappeared into the offices. Alex said, "This may be a false alarm – but better safe than sorry, of course! All we can do now is wait! You ladies can all go and have a cup of tea and a bun in the café if you want, and Jimmy and I will keep watch in case Mal wants anything and to make sure no visitors try to go in."

"Not on your life!" said Melpomene, "I don't want to miss anything – how about you, Marjorie and Winnie?"

"Us neither!" said Winnie, "What's the point of working for detectives if you're going to skip all the fun and excitement!"

Nothing at all happened for over an hour.

Then Jimmy looked once again at this watch and said, "I'm all out of gossip – I'm going to creep up the stairs and call to Mal through the open door – I won't blunder in unless Mal gives me the OK."

Then he reappeared on the stairs and called, "It's all clear now, you can all come up, but stay in the outer office and Mal will tell us what he's been up to."

When they were all assembled, Mal said, "No need to take notes, ladies and gentlemen, but I shall now give you the first introductory lesson in bomb disposal – suspicious parcels division. Point 1: never, never, never, cut the string round a dodgy parcel before you have checked it thoroughly! And the reason for this is that it might be holding down a spring trigger of some sort."

"So what can you do?" asked Melpomene.

"First, you carefully feel the entire brown wrapper to see what you can discover beneath it – again it might be holding down a trigger. Oh, by the way, I asked whether the courier was handling it gingerly, because some devices are sensitive to shock and vibration – this one apparently was not. Once you have checked for these triggers, you can proceed to remove the string and carefully peel back the brown paper. I did this and found that the parcel consisted of two flat tins that had once contained Farrah's Harrogate Toffee, one much heavier than the other, which, with some trepidation I must admit, I opened. It was full of sand! So I now had to decide what to do about the other, much lighter tin. I shook it gently, to see whether it rattled, but it didn't, so I carefully prised up one corner of the lid and peeped in – I was wearing these safety glasses which workmen use when they are grinding metal objects."

The entire audience was holding its collective breath. Mal continued.

"All I could see was an off-white powder, which ruled out an explosive or incendiary device, so I immediately closed the tin again, and went and washed my hands."

"So you thought it might be poisonous!" said Alex.

"That was certainly one possibility – so the next step is to send it off to the Lambeth police lab to see whether they can identify it. It could be a poisonous substance, or something that will spread a disease – I've heard of anthrax spores being sent in letters to infect the recipient. We shan't know until tests have been done – I'll alert the lab to the possibility, but they're pretty much on the ball anyway! Have you got any parcel tape I can use to seal up the tin before I send it? And I'll take all the wrapping for fingerprint checks – I was wearing gloves all the time, of course."

Marjorie said, "Thanks for the lesson, Sergeant, and for saving all our lives! You deserve several cups of tea and some snacks now!"

While they were enjoying the tea and jam tarts, Alex said, "We mustn't overlook the fact that the parcel was addressed to 'Melpommy Musgrave' – the last people who made this spelling mistake were Elspeth McCracken and Henry Jackson, but even they found out the correct spelling along the line, and to the bargain now they are both locked up. They may have made arrangements for the parcel some days ago, but without knowing the name of the courier firm it's hard to check."

Jimmy said, "We only grabbed Jackson a couple of days ago, but as you pointed out, he now knows the correct spelling of 'Melpomene', so it is unlikely he was the one who sent the parcel. I think I'll put Cec Thomson onto a hunt among the motorbike courier services – there can't be all that many of them, since it's only a recent development. If we can find the person who sent the parcel, this will give us another lead into the whole criminal organisation, if it really exists."

"The indications are," said Mel, "that there are medical connections involved here, whether or not the powder turns out to be a bacteriological agent or a toxin. These are not the approaches one might expect a mob of stand-over thugs to take – much too sophisticated, I would say."

Alex added, "And what I'm wondering about is this – if it turns out to be anthrax or some other bacteriological agent – where does one obtain such substances? Would Vanessa Spring be able to make suggestions? She is in the field and she has connections with the Microbiology people at University College, too."

"Once we get something back from the lab, we can explore that avenue," said Jimmy, "and if instead it's some chemical poison, or drug, there are plenty of people around that would be able to get anything of that nature through their suppliers in the pharmacology trade. Did you say, Alex, that you intended to visit Mr Stephenson at Katzenberg's shortly? You would have to be even more careful with questions since today's incident!"

Chapter 49

"We'll let you know as soon as we have more information about the white powder," said Jimmy as he and Mal left the office to go back to Mile End Road "one of our motorcycle couriers will take it to the Lambeth lab – oh, there's a thought, maybe they would know about the commercial courier firms, so I'll ask."

When they had gone, Mel asked Marjorie, "Amongst all the other exciting mail today, was there a summons to the Coroner's Court?"

"Oh yes, you're both required to attend at noon tomorrow."

"Good, that'll give us a chance to do some telephoning in the morning – I have a few people in mind," said Melpomene, "but right now I'll ring Mama – she'll be shocked but thrilled to hear about our 'bomb'!"

"And while you're doing that," said Alex, "I shall see whether Mr Stephenson can see me tomorrow morning. I want to see whether he has had any reaction from Beestlers in Luxembourg."

A woman answered him and said "Minerva Watts here, how can I help?" When Alex introduced himself as Alan Robertson and asked for Stephenson, she said, with what sounded like a catch in her voice, "Mr Stephenson is no longer with us – Katzenberg's is in the hands of the official receivers now and he has been taken into custody – I'm not allowed to say any more!"

Once Mel was off the other telephone, Alex told everybody about this and said, "This probably means that the authorities may also have descended on Dalgleish and McDonald's – I wonder whether there will be ramifications in Luxembourg for Beestler's? It depends on the shareholders really – we can only assume that the receivers have been called in by them. If we keep our eye on the financial pages of the Times, we might get some idea, but these matters are often zealously guarded, so we may never know the full story. When we see Philip Seaward next time he will probably be able to explain all these things. I'll telephone him tomorrow and find out when he's going to be allowed into the hospital to do his stuff."

Melpomene then said, "I don't know about all of you people, but I'm really keyed up after all today's happenings, and I think I need something to take my mind off them for a while. What say we go to the pictures tonight, all of us, and finish off at a good restaurant? There are posters at the local cinema advertising the latest Douglas Fairbanks movie, 'The Gaucho', with Mary Pickford and that new glamourous star from Mexico, Lupe Vélez. Who's with me?"

Everybody was in favour, so a little later they trooped into the cinema for the evening performance and took their seats, not too near the screen, just as the curtains parted and the image of a rooster announced the British Pathé newsreel, showing two women and a man preparing to swim the Channel, a military parade in India, and two or three sporting events, ending with a piece about students at Harpenden University sitting down in protest against unfair admission practices – as far as one could judge from their banners.

The main feature was well worth the wait, and was discussed with great animation round the restaurant table as they enjoyed their meal. Winifred and Marjorie liked Douglas Fairbanks, and Alex pretended to be indifferent, while Mel grinned inwardly as she recollected his rapt expression whenever Señorita Vélez was on the screen.

The next morning, Mel and Alex decided to go to the office straight after breakfast, since there were two telephone lines there and the both wanted to make several calls.

As they arrived, Winnie was talking on the telephone and she beckoned Alex to take it, saying, "It's Jimmy, he's got the lab results!" Melpomene picked up the second earpiece to listen as well, hearing Jimmy say, "The laboratory workers first suspected that the powder was anthrax spores, which are extremely dangerous and can be inhaled easily, but fortunately – or comparatively so – it turned out to be powdered ricin. This is still dangerous – it is a poison extracted from castor-oil beans – but spreads much less easily. If anyone had touched it, they may have been badly affected, all the same. We are lucky that Mel's antennae are so sensitive! Now, the next step is to trace the parcel's sender – once we find him or her there will be a *prima facie* case for assault with a deadly weapon."

"How about fingerprints?" asked Alex.

"If he or they are sophisticated enough to use ricin like this, they would probably know enough to avoid leaving prints. Our best bet is to track them through the courier. Our motorbike people are putting together a list for us, and then Cec or one of his mates will try tracking him down."

"That's very encouraging, Jimmy!" said Alex, "Have you heard when the hospital offices will be released for our auditor to go in?"

"Good you reminded me, Alex – I'll get onto our forensics people as soon as I ring off – last time I spoke to them they were saying that they should be signing off on the place this morning, and would give Mr Seaward the go-ahead then. Perhaps it would be quicker if you ring him directly, and then you can check whether he wants you go in with him."

When he rang off, Mel was talking on the other line, so he waited until she hung up.

"That was Vanessa," she said, "as soon as I heard that the white powder was ricin, I thought I would ask her if she had any idea where someone might lay their hands on quantities of the stuff – but she said that there were no commercial sources of ricin itself, but that anyone could grow castor oil beans in a pot on the window-sill and extract the ricin in their kitchen if they knew how, so we should hunt down whoever sent it instead. I was astounded to hear that the plant is commonly grown in gardens because it is very decorative! And after we had discussed that, she said that we might be approached on a completely different matter by a friend of hers – something to do with improper procedures for admission to a university where she's applying to do a PhD. She gave her friend, who is called Angela Dayton, our address and telephone number."

"Interesting!" said Alex, "Were you still listening when Jimmy said we should ring Philip Seaward about going with him to see the burnt-out offices at the hospital?"

"Yes, you'd better do that now, because we shall have to be going to the inquest before long, and I need several cups of tea and a jam tart to fortify myself first!"

Philip Seaward said there was no immediate hurry – he and an assistant would be arriving there at about ten the next day and would meet them at the hospital – they should bring overalls, because there could be layers of oily soot on everything!

Chapter 50

In the event, the inquest went off surprisingly smoothly. Dr Aitcheson confirmed that, based on the results he had now received from the blood tests, the lady's death was indeed due to an overdose of barbiturates. Neither Melpomene nor Alex were required to testify, and Jimmy Manley substantiated the claim by Douglas Latham and his dispenser, Edwin Stringer, that the supply of the wrong strength Donnatal tablets was entirely due to poor labelling by the wholesaler. The coroner, Dr Wilfred Collins, rebuked Dr Lewis for vagueness in prescribing, but acknowledged that, even with his error, had the prescription been filled as written, no harm would have come to Mrs Pratt-Smithers. Summing up, he returned a verdict of 'death by misadventure', but made a strong recommendation that a investigation be made by the police to discover whether any employee of the suppliers might be found culpable over the labelling error.

Jimmy and the other policemen went back to their station, leaving Mel, Alex, Gordon Salmon and Dr Aitcheson to adjourn to a neighbouring pub and discuss the proceedings over a ploughman's lunch and a beer or two. As he left, Jimmy said he would celebrate with them later, when he had come off duty, saying, "We think we've tracked down the chief arsonist, too, but we have to interrogate him further. I'll ring your office, Mel and Alex, when I'm sure of my facts – hopefully this afternoon!"

Back at the office, Marjorie and Winnie of course demanded a full account of the inquest, and Melpomene had hardly finished relating it, with the use of gestures and appropriate voices for all the participants, when the telephone rang and Jimmy Manley announced that he and Cec Thomson were on their way, arriving shortly afterwards.

"I can't remember," Jimmy said, as he accepted a cup of tea, "whether I've told you already about the people who took advantage of young Peter Parsons at the dairy. Anyway we picked up the driver, going by the name of Clark, who'd left his prints all over the phenolphthalein tin – his name is Paul Andrew Timmins and he's been known to us for ages, so we had no real trouble finding him. As for his companion, alias Challis, Cec and I took Mrs Parsons, Peter's mum, to

Katzenberg's and, all innocently, asked to speak to someone who deals with local businesses. The girl we spoke to said she would ask Mr Houghton, and he came out of his office. As soon as he and Mrs Parsons came face to face, all the blood drained from his face, as she said, 'That's Mr Challis!' – so we grabbed him and gave him a new pair of bracelets!"

"You mentioned the arsonist, too, this morning!" said Melpomene, "Did you find him as well?"

"Strangely enough, we already had him in custody – Dean Jackson, as you like to call him! I was questioning him on his relationship with Elspeth McCracken, and I arranged for Cec Thomson to come into the interview room and say 'Just to let you know, Inspector, I heard that the man who suffered the bad burns at the scene of the hospital fire has passed away, poor guy!' This produced a satisfactory result, from our point of view, anyway – Jackson almost fainted and blurted out, 'I never wanted this – who will break it to his wife and children?' So I took the opportunity to ask him directly about his part in the arson – he admitted to it without further ado!"

"We'll see you at the hospital tomorrow, when we see how Philip Seaward copes with the burnt-out office." said Alex, "He advised us to wear overalls."

Melpomene and Alex were waiting at the door of the finance office when Philip and his assistant, who he introduced as Steve Conway, arrived closely followed by Jimmy, who unlocked the door and ushered them in. The atmosphere was still oppressive, with the mingled smells of smoke and petrol, but there was some breeze coming in through the broken windows.

The room contained, as well as rows of filing cabinets, two desks, one with a typewriter and both with telephones – all of them blackened and distorted. Philip went over and pulled open the top drawer of a cabinet with some difficulty. He took out a file folder and put it on the desk.

"Let's see," he said, "it doesn't look too bad to me!" and he opened it. The papers inside had scorched edges and were stained, but seemed to be reasonably legible.

"Unless the water from the firemen's hoses has flooded into any of these, we should be able to get what we want from them! The water damage in this first one looks as though it's just due to a trickle getting in through the gaps. As I told you before, I think, it would take a very intense fire to destroy papers in folders like these. Well, unless any of you really wants to watch or even help, Steve and I will just get on with it. Perhaps you could ask for teas and snacks to be brought in after a couple of hours – it'll take us two or three days altogether, I'd judge."

As Mel, Alex and Jimmy thanked him and left, a woman approached them, saying, "Mr and Mrs Crabbe and Inspector Manley? Please come and meet the chairman and members of the Hospital Board."

She took them along a corridor and showed them into a room where there were a number of people, including Gordon Salmon, Dr Aitcheson and Matron Stevenson standing around drinking coffee or tea, and announced them. A silver-haired, rather portly gentleman came forward, saying, "I am Sir Michael Vestey, ex-Commodore of the Royal Navy, and I have the honour of chairing this Board. I have already met Detective-Inspector Manley, so you must be Melpomene and Alexander Crabbe – I welcome you with great pleasure!"

He shook hands with all three, and showed them to chairs at the large oval table, seating them at each side of his own place.

"Without any more ado, "he announced, "I shall come straight to business. I and this Board extend to you our heartfelt thanks for the work you have accomplished on behalf of this hospital, and indeed for the community it serves. We shall not know the full extent to which our erstwhile employees, Miss McCracken and Mr Jackson and their confederates, have been robbing us over the years until Mr Seaward and his firm have completed their audit, but by all estimates the amount has been substantial – to say nothing of the attempt to burn us down! Consequently, the Board has agreed, *nemine contradicente*, to reward your agency, Crabbe and Crabbe, with a sum that accords with the benefit that you have bestowed upon us through your expert and diligent work. Please accept this cheque along with our heartfelt thanks! We should also not let the opportunity pass to congratulate Inspector Manley and the other members of the Metropolitan Police on their sterling work. Now, I think, the sun being over the yard-arm, as they say, let us all drink a toast to the successful completion of this enterprise – I acknowledge that there still remain a few untied ends!"

Champagne was served, and conversation proceeded happily for over an hour, until Melpomene and Alex called for a taxi!

KEEP VIGILANT FOR THE NEXT CASE!

Crabbe and Crabbe's next case will be coming out soon!

Will there be murders? Who knows.

Will there be skulduggery? Undoubtedly.

Will Melpomene and Alex solve the case?

Of course – how could anyone doubt this!

Look out for:

"An Academic Question"

A Case for Crabbe and Crabbe.

By Geoffrey Foster

Coming in a few months.